Flirt

Black Hawk MC
Book Seven

by Carson Mackenzie

Published by CM Books, LLC
Copyright © March 2021 Carson Mackenzie
Cover Design by Carson Mackenzie
Cover Images Licensed for Use: Deposit Photos
ISBN# 978-1-952184-03-1 Digital
ISBN# 978-1-952184-05-5 PB
ISBN# 978-1-952184-37-6 PB
ISBN# 978-1-666269-35-2 PB

Synopsis

Max "Flirt" Browning has watched a group of men he considers more than club brothers take the plunge into family life. As the last man standing, he's not opposed to following them—he's just never found the right woman. At least not before Brie walked into his life.

With her, he could see a future. Getting her to see that he was interested in more than a couple of sexual encounters a month could cost every ounce of control Flirt possessed. The control he needed as much as the air he breathes. For her—he'd do whatever it took.

Gabriella "Brie" Agassi has had to manage every aspect of her life, from raising a daughter to building a pediatric practice. With not much free time to pursue a relationship—and considering when she tried, it had been one disastrous date after another—she takes matters into her own hands and visits Whispering Nights.

At the club, she'd find a take-charge man to whom she could relinquish total sexual control for an hour or two. Giving her the break needed from her responsibilities to bring balance back into her life. Balance she hasn't had since her fiancé died.

Meeting Max Browning, Brie wondered how much her need for balance was going to cost her. And if she'd be willing or able to pay the price.

Message from the Author

Parts of Flirt's book runs consecutively time wise to Coast's storyline. To do his story justice, we needed to know what Flirt had been up to while Coast was working his magic on Mackenzie.

Table of Contents

Prologue

Flirt

For the first time since I came home from the military and became a member of Whispering Nights, I felt disconcerted as I walked through the doors. Not sure why I had come in the first place, though deep down, I knew the reason behind my unrest. I just wasn't ready to voice it out loud.

As I took a seat at the bar, Rudy, the bartender for the night, placed my usual down in front of me. I lifted my chin in acknowledgment and thanks and picked up the chilled bottle of water, twisting the cap. He returned the gesture, then moved down to wait on a Dom and his sub sitting at the other end of the bar.

"How are you this evening, Max?" Mark Baker, the owner of Whispering Nights, asked as he sat down on the vacant stool beside me.

Reaching over, I shook Mark's hand. "Doing good. How about you?" I asked.

"Could be better, my friend," he said with a chuckle.

Lifting a brow, I inquired, "Should I bother asking if you want or need to talk about it?"

I met Mark while going through the NCP (Navy College Program). Mark had been a PO1 (Petty Officer First Class) and was interested in a getting a college degree before ending his time in the Navy while I was a Seaman Recruit. I wanted to get a degree to advance myself through the ranks. We talked while we waited to be seen by a counselor and discovered we were both from the state of Washington.

Despite the fifteen plus years' age difference, Mark and I quickly become friends.

During the times between taking online classes and my training to become a Navy SEAL, I'd been more than grateful for the friendship he and I shared. Especially when I found myself at the lowest, mentally, and physically. Drained to the point, I allowed doubt to seep into my mind, wondering if I could complete either task. Mark had been there to give me the much-needed pep talk. His verbal shoves never failed to set me back on course.

It had taken me longer to get the business degree than to complete all the training required to become a deployable SEAL. Thirty months total for the mandatory training by the Navy. In the end, the time and effort I'd put in had been worth it.

Mark had also been the one who introduced me to an alternate lifestyle. He invited me as a guest to the place he frequented as a member. It had been during one of my weakest moments as a Seaman Recruit when the stress had weighed heavily on my shoulders. He'd witnessed my struggles and suggested the club might be just what I was looking for. I went out of curiosity. Not sure if watching people satisfy their kink was for me. I'd experienced nothing like it, though. The atmosphere, the sexual tempo, watching a few scenes play out, it called to a part of me I never knew existed. It was as if a piece of me clicked into place. After that day, I never looked back. I embraced the controlling side of me. Before, I'd controlled every part of my life but the sexual side. Sex had just been about obtaining a release. I'd had no idea there was so much missing—more satisfaction for my sexual partner and for me.

"I served in the Navy for twenty-two years, and I've been a Dom for well over thirty. A big part of being good at both is the ability to read people, anticipate the needs of the ones in my care. But damn it all if my ten-month-old daughter doesn't make me feel like a fraud."

I chuckled at his expression and the fact that one of the best men I knew seemed distraught over his inability to handle his young daughter.

"Glad you find it amusing," he griped and rubbed his hand down his face before he continued. "Christ, I've had sailors tear up during a dressing down. Chrissy, she only needs to look at me and bat her eyes, and I crumble. And if I see a tear, I'm toast."

It felt good to focus on someone else's problem, if only for a few minutes. "Come on, Mark. She's ten months. You're her daddy, isn't it her job to wrap you around her finger?"

Mark and his wife, Stella, had been married a little over twelve years. They'd given up on trying for a family after going through every test and every suggestion the doctors made to help them conceive, no matter how slim the chance. Nothing had worked for them. After giving up on having a child, a year later Stella became pregnant, and I had never seen a couple more ecstatic. Mark looked happier and physically relaxed the day he had shared the news.

"Oh yeah, speaks the man with no kids. Nothing in life prepares us for children. And I mean nothing. There are no instructions for becoming a parent. The entire deal redefines on-the-job training. Oh, as adults, we think we can handle them because we read a bunch of books. How hard can it be, right? Besides, we're bigger and stronger than they are. But I'm thinking they are so much smarter. For God's sake, Stella ran to the store the other day, and left me home alone with Chrissy. I left her playing on the floor in the living room for one minute while I stepped into the kitchen to get myself something to drink. I walked back into the room, and she had a paperback of Stella's tearing pages out and depositing the pieces into the vent on the floor. A minute, man. I'm not even sure how she got the paperback off the side table. When I tried scolding her, she looked up at me, batted her little eyes, and then grinned."

"I have faith in you. You'll get fatherhood down... eventually," I said while chuckling.

"Like I have any other choice. That little girl doesn't listen to me at all. Even if I raise my voice. Stella is enjoying it immensely." Mark shook his head, sighed, then went on. "Enough about the issues I'm having with my women. Tell me what's been going on with you and your brothers. I haven't seen you around lately. Catch me up. I need a distraction from my own life."

"The bike business is good. Steady stream of orders. My brothers are pretty much like you—either dealing with their ol' ladies or dealing with tiny females with attitudes," I answered and grinned at the thought of Ally, Neely and Poppy. "Jag and River tied the knot last weekend at the clubhouse. Nothing too exciting happening otherwise."

"Leaves you and Coast the last two holdouts, huh? A lot has changed since you guys made it home," Mark said, and I waited to reply until Rudy was walking away after setting down a glass in front of Mark. I didn't have to guess what the glass contained. Mark drank nothing but club soda when he was at the club.

12

"It depends if Coast catches the dodging doctor, then he won't be unattached much longer," I said as I rolled the bottle between my hands and listened to the plastic crinkle. I knew it was a nervous gesture and forced myself to stop.

Mark touched my shoulder. "Let's go talk in my office, Max," he said, drank his glass empty, then stood from his barstool. I lifted the bottle of water to my mouth and finished it, then placed the empty bottle on the bar before I rose and followed him.

Once we were in his office, he waved for me to take a seat in one of the two chairs in front of his desk. After I sat in one, Mark sat beside me in the other one instead of going behind his desk.

"What's really going on with you, Max? I know you, friend. Something's bothering you."

"What do you mean? I just told you," I replied and frowned.

His brow cocked, and he looked at me as he relaxed back in the chair. "Maybe I should be the one asking, *Do you want or need to talk about it?*"

I ran a hand down my face and contemplated how much to say to Mark. I could easily have stuck with nothing being wrong, but I respected Mark too much to blow him off. Not to mention the man had always been able to read me.

I took a deep breath. It seemed I would voice my feelings of late whether or not I was ready, then blew it out. "I'm questioning my participation in the club. It's lost some of its appeal. I've always enjoyed the ability to help a sub reach subspace where pleasure overrides and nothing else matters. Watch them fall, then use my experience to comfort and soothe until they're back in control of their emotions. Lately, though, I am unfulfilled."

"Is that why you've been scarce around here?" Mark asked, and I nodded.

"Yes. I thought a break might refresh me. I grew tired of walking away disappointed in myself. Hell, you mentioned being a fraud. Maybe I've been the fraud all along." I hated discussing my own feelings. It sucked and made me sound like a whiny asshole.

"Being dominant isn't something you can shut on and off, Max, but you know that already. I know you've never had a desire to be connected to one sub. However, maybe that is what's changed, my friend."

I opened my mouth to speak, and Mark held his hand up.

"Let me finish. Before Stella, I was the same way. Oh, it's fun and satisfying to have the control and skills to know what the sub in front of you needs just from their body language. For some of us, it grows monotonous over time because, outside of playing, we never form a deep connection with anyone. When I retired and came back and opened this place, I wasn't looking for a D/s relationship that went past the inside of a club. At least until Stella showed up. Maybe wanting a connection is subconsciously driving what you're experiencing."

"I've witnessed the connection and bond between you and some of the other Doms with their subs. There's balance in your relationships. Along the way, I lost mine. I'm not sure I even had it to begin with. I'm not finding it here at Whispering Nights."

Mark gave me a half-smile. "I'm not going to say you're wrong. No one can decide that but you. I think you're lonely."

"Lonely?" I shook my head and guffawed. "You have to be alone to be lonely. Which I never am. Hell, I haven't been alone since the day I was born. Have you forgotten I'm

14

surrounded by MC brothers? Have you forgotten my time in the Navy?"

"Not hardly. But people can still surround you, making you feel lonely at the same time. You know that, too. You can't tell me there weren't times even on a ship with thousands of sailors, you hadn't experienced loneliness. I felt it on more than one occasion throughout my career in the service. There are differences, Max. You referenced the bond and commitment we in the club have with our subs or wives. Do you not see the same between your MC brothers and their ol' ladies?"

I took a deep breath, then blew it out. "My brothers share the same," I answered while I rubbed a hand across the back of my neck. "Christ, I feel as if I should lie on a couch."

Mark chuckled. "I'm far from a therapist, and I'm sure if you spoke with Stella, she'd inform you I could still improve on my listening skills."

"Stella would say nothing negative about you. Even if it was true." I regarded my friend and turned over everything he said before I continued. "So, you're telling me that what I'm feeling amounts to jealousy of what you and my brothers have found with your women? Do you know how fucked up it sounds? I'm happy for them and you. The women you've found are awesome, and they fit."

"Not jealousy, Max. Balance. Balance isn't exclusive to the D/s relationship. It is in every aspect of our lives. You've watched your brothers find the women who balance them. Strengthen them and complete them. They accept them, flaws and all. Same as they do for their women. Same as Stella does for me. Unlike you, I never had the feeling I was missing anything in my life. Not until I met Stella. Then I wondered how I survived so long without her. I'd wager it was the same with your brothers."

"I've never run from commitment. Not with the Navy, the MC, or any aspects dealing with my personal life. I've mentioned countless times to my brothers that if I found the right woman for me, there'd be no denying it or fighting the fact. And if she needed a push, I'd tie her to my bed until she realized I was everything she needed or was looking for."

I frowned when Mark burst out laughing. "Oh, you, my friend, are going to go down hard when you cross paths with the right woman."

"I highly doubt that."

"I don't, my friend. We like having control and structure in our lives. The need of the two for us is like the need for air. It doesn't matter what type of relationship you have with your partner. If they're happy, you're happy. Bet your brothers prefer their women happy, too. Life goes a little smoother when they are."

"Oh, my brothers would definitely agree with you there." I stood. "Thanks for the talk, Mark. I think I will head back to Black Hawk. I'm not feeling it tonight."

Mark stood, and we shook hands. "I'm headed home myself after my meeting."

"Shit, I've been in my head so much, I didn't even ask about Stella. Is she here?"

"Stella's doing great. She's at home with Chrissy tonight. I only showed up to meet with a potential new sub." Mark looked at his watch. "As a matter of fact, she should be here any minute."

"Well, I'll leave you to it." I walked to the door and opened it.

"You can hang around and be the welcoming committee." We both walked out into the hallway.

"There are plenty here tonight to help you out. You shouldn't have a problem finding any volunteers. You know us unattached Doms can smell a new submissive from a hundred yards." I chuckled. "Besides, the mood I've been in might scare her off."

"True. Especially since she's unsure of being a submissive, but if a club is what she's actually looking for."

I ran my fingers through my hair. "New to everything?" I asked as I pulled my fingers from my hair and waved my arm out. "Does she have a clue what goes on in a club? This isn't a store where you check out the items offered, then if you like them, you make a purchase. What the hell?"

"Wow, you really are struggling right now. Do you think I would bother vetting her if I thought she was just curious?"

I dropped my arm to my side, took a deep breath, and blew it out. "No." I definitely needed to get back to the compound, go in my house, and shut the world out until my attitude improved.

"Gabriella is submissive. She may not know for sure, but after speaking with her, I know."

Whispering Nights wasn't an 'open to the public' club. It was exclusive, and it vetted potential members before they signed a contract or paid any fees. Even when a member wanted to bring a guest, they had to be cleared first.

All unattached submissives were only known in the club by their first names. They wore colored bracelets to signify their standing in the club. Unattached subs' colors represented their standing, but also differentiated a sub's level of kink. Something they would have filled out on their original paperwork under hard limits.

"We all started somewhere," I said as we walked toward the main room.

"Yes, we did. I'm sure she'll have no issue finding a Dom to help her get adjusted."

I looked at Mark and lifted a brow. "New and inexperienced? Seriously, that didn't even need to be said. They'll line up to train her."

"She admitted having trouble telling her partners what she needs which, by the way, totals three. She chalked her problem up to inexperience, then admitted she read a few BDSM romances and—"

I stopped walking and looked at my friend. "Are you fucking kidding me? What? She reads a few books and decides playing out a few sex scenes sounded fun."

Mark snorted. "No, the books opened her eyes and made her realize things about herself. One being the feeling of needing more sexually isn't always because of inexperience or a partner's inability to please you. Sometimes, it's finding…," Mark smirked. "Balance."

I groaned. "Now I wish I hadn't talked with you."

"Please, you live for our talks."

It was my turn to snort. "Sure, it is like looking forward to an annual prostate exam."

"You're such a dickhead," Mark said and laughed. "Seriously though, maybe you should stick around. When I'm finished meeting with Gabriella, I was going to have Sonny show her around tonight. Why don't you stay and do it? Who knows, you might find what you're missing."

"Tell me you are not attempting to play matchmaker," I said and glared at my friend.

Mark slapped me on the shoulder. Not fazed at my tone. "You never know. She could be the one you're looking for, and she'll be snapped up by one of the others before you have time to meet her."

"I'll have to take the chance and deal with the outcome." I rested my hand on Mark's shoulder and squeezed. "It was good running into you. I'll catch you later." I dropped my hand, then took the last few steps to the set of doors that would lead me to the entrance area where the security/check-in desk was.

After I told Nate, who was manning the desk, to have a good night, I made my way to the set of doors that would take me out of the club and into the parking lot. As I reached for the handle, the door swung open, and I shifted to the side as a brunette hurriedly brushed past with a "Sorry" thrown over her shoulder.

Holding the door partially open to prepare for leaving, I watched the woman make her way to the counter where Nate stood watching her approach. The scent of her perfume lingered around me, and the sway of her hips held me in place. She was quite the package, and I briefly wished I had gotten a look at her face.

Then I remembered the crappy mood I was in and turned back to the outside. I had just taken a step when she spoke, "Hi, I'm supposed to meet Mark… I mean Master Mark. I'm Gabriella," in a throaty voice that stroked down my entire body.

I froze for a split second and weighed how much grief I was willing to take from Mark. I stepped back and let the door close, then turned and walked toward the counter. With my approach, the woman turned her head and looked up at me.

When I made contact with her dark brown eyes, I suddenly didn't give a damn. Whatever Mark dished out; I would take. Looking into her eyes, I had a feeling it would be worth it.

"Welcome to Whispering Nights, Gabriella."

"Umm… thank you. And you are?"

One corner of my mouth lifted. "I'm hoping soon… Sir."

Chapter One

Flirt

As I crawled out from under my dad's cabin, I continued to breathe through my mouth until I was free from the confined space and able to stand, then I inhaled deeply and blew it out. I left the garbage bag I'd dragged out with me on the ground and handed my dad the flashlight I had used while underneath his place.

"Leave the crawl space door open to air out the stench from under there," I said as I bent and tried dusting some of the dirt from my jeans.

"What's in the bag?" Romeo, my dad, asked.

"A raccoon. From the look of it, it's been dead for a little while." I straightened and pulled the work gloves off my hands and shoved the tops in my back pocket. Glad I thought to grab them on my way out of the house after answering the call from my dad.

"Well, how did the bastard get under there in the first place?"

"I have no clue, but you're lucky Claire's got a sensitive nose. If that raccoon stayed under there any longer, the smell would have seeped into the cabin and been intolerable." I reached down and grabbed the twisted top of the bag, lifting it. "You want me to toss this in the dumpster at the clubhouse?"

"Yeah, probably better than stuffing it in my trash can," my dad said as we started walking around to the front of his place. When we reached the front where my truck was parked, I tossed the bag in the bed.

"You want to come inside and have dinner with Claire and me? Pot roast."

"Thanks for the invite, but I ate right before you called. Besides, I want to get home and clean up," I said and reached in my pocket and pulled out my keys.

"Probably ate a sandwich, and that isn't a meal. And I know you aren't worried about tracking in a little dirt. So, why the rush?"

I snorted and pulled the driver's side door open. "Until Claire, you ate sandwiches more than once for dinner."

"Now I don't have to. Well, unless she works late at the bakery."

I reached out and patted my dad's stomach. Knowing underneath the t-shirt his stomach was still flat, I teased, "Yeah, eating those desserts for dinner are showing."

"You're full of shit and a smartass," Dad said, then slapped my arm. "But thanks for coming over and crawling under the cabin."

"No problem. You shouldn't be under there, anyway; I bumped my head a few times, getting from one side to the other. Not a lot of moveability space for an old man like you."

"Claire doesn't seem to have a problem with how I move."

"Christ, now I know it's time for me to go," I said and got into my truck. "You better not let Claire hear you say stuff like that, or the only thing you'll be moving is your hand up and down," I added as I reached for the handle on the door.

"Please, the woman can't keep her hands off me."

I snorted. "Old and delusional." Instead of laughing or coming back with his own smart-ass remark, my dad frowned and reached inside and clasped the back of my neck with his hand.

"All joking aside. Besides having you as a son, Claire's the best thing to happen to me. Don't wait until you're my age to experience life with a good woman by your side." Dad squeezed my neck, dropped his hand, and stepped back from the opening of my truck door.

"Everything alright with you, Dad?"

"Sure, never better. I couldn't be happier."

Focused on my dad and knowing his tells, he wasn't just giving the blanketed response with his facial expressions and body language. Since hooking up with Claire, he was happier than I had ever seen him, and I trusted that if anything was up with his health, he would let me know.

"Alright. I'm out of here," I said as I grabbed the driver's side door handle just in time to hold on to it as a gust of wind pushed against it. It reminded me of the earlier weather report I caught on the television. "There is the possibility of a storm tonight. Make sure you and the other dads have your generators filled. Might end up needing them."

"We took care of ours a couple of weeks ago. Even fired them up to make sure they were working well."

"Good. Have a good evening with Claire. I'll catch you later." My dad moved toward his front door after I closed my door. I started the truck, then turned it around and headed toward the other side of the compound where the others and I lived.

It had taken less than five minutes for me to drop the trash bag in the club's dumpster before I was pulling up to the unattached garage behind my house.

I hit the remote and opened one of the bay doors, but instead of driving into the garage, I parked the truck outside. I would drive it when I left for Whispering Nights on the off chance the weatherman was wrong in his reporting about the storm not arriving until much later in the night.

Why take the chance of getting caught in a rainstorm on my bike when I could avoid it from the beginning?

As I reached my hand to hit the remote to close the garage door, the light inside flickered. I got out of my truck and, taking the advice I had given my dad, headed to check my generator. On my way into the garage, I pulled out my phone and texted my brothers to remind them they might want to do the same with theirs. The only brother not included in the text was Coast. I had noticed the inside of his house was as dark as mine when I drove up.

Coast was no doubt in hot pursuit of Mac, so with no clue to when he would make it home, I crossed the yard to his place and took care of his generator first.

Once I had taken care of both generators and made sure they would operate adequately if we lost power, I headed inside my house to shower. It was the first time in quite a while that I looked forward to going to Whispering Nights. I knew it had everything to do with Gabriella. Since my first encounter with her two weeks ago at the club, she was all I had thought about. That night she had strolled past me, leaving the lingering scent of her perfume surrounding me. Everything about her had appealed to me, but it was when she spoke, the sound of her voice had me turning toward her. The throaty, husky tone had caused an effect on my entire body. It was then I knew I would do whatever it took to have her.

After Nate, the security officer behind the desk, notified Mark of her arrival, I immediately volunteered to escort her inside. I placed my hand on the small of her back and led her into the club. Mark had stood inside the doors, and when he saw me with Gabriella, his lips twitched. A sure sign the next time he and I were alone, he would have plenty to say.

Once Mark had greeted her, he gave another glance to me, then informed Gabriella that I would show her around the club.

Our tour started with the main floor area where the Doms and their subs played openly for all interested in watching. As we circled the area, her calm composure made it easy to forget she was new to everything going on around her. Well, at least until we reached the area Master Thomas and his submissive, Danielle, were occupying. The whiz of the bullwhip could be heard and was what stopped Gabriella in her tracks.

We stood at the edge of the group already formed and took in the scene. I kept my focus on Gabriella instead of Master Thomas' skill. He was one of two Masters at Whispering Heights who were experts with the bullwhip. Master Thomas even held beginner classes for any Dom or Domme who wished to learn.

With every contact of the whip on Danielle's skin, Gabriella's composure slipped. I moved closer to her, to where my hand brushed against her arm. I noticed her chest rise and fall as her breathing picked up, and I wondered if it was because of my closeness or what was playing out in front of us. When I saw a blush form on Gabriella's cheeks, I turned my head toward Master Thomas and Danielle. By the look in Danielle's eyes, she had reached the coveted subspace, and Master Thomas had stopped, laid the whip aside, and unfastened the front of his pants. When he entered Danielle with one thrust of his hips, I heard Gabriella's intake of air and turned to find her staring at me. I wrapped my hand around her arm and slid it down to her wrist, her pulse rapidly beating as we started moving away to continue with the tour.

I was yanked from the thoughts of my first meeting with Gabriella when the water in the shower turned cold. I shook my head and finished rinsing off, then turned off the shower, stepped out onto the bathmat, grabbed the bath towel off the rack, and dried off quickly. While I finished the rest of my bathroom rituals, I kept thoughts of Gabriella at bay.

"Christ, the anticipation of being near her. Mixed with the excitement of having her submit to me, I'll be surprised if I don't shoot my load before I even get inside her," I said as I opened my closet door and walked in. The sooner I dressed and left—the sooner I would get to the club. And if I were lucky, I would have time for a drink before Gabriella showed up. Something I never did unless it involved water. However, if I were going to make Gabriella's first active experience as a submissive count, I would need a swig of liquor to settle myself.

"Fuck, the woman is already making me want to drink. And evidently talk to myself," I said as I walked down the stairs, stopped and grabbed my plain leather jacket from the hall closet, then headed to the kitchen.

Since I never wore my vest or anything Black Hawk MC related to Whispering Nights, my vest hung on the back of a kitchen chair. I shoved my cell in one of the jacket pockets and grabbed the keys off the counter. When I stepped out the back door, I noticed Coast pull up to his garage. I locked my door and turned toward his place and started across the yard.

"Yo!" I yelled and saw Mac jump, then Coast placed his arm around her, pulling her closer. "Sorry, Mackenzie. I didn't mean to scare you," I added as I stepped into view.

"It's okay. I didn't see you. It's pretty dark out here, even with the house lights on. Plus, I have noticed none of you men make noise when you walk," Mackenzie said as I walked up. Emery and I both chuckled at her remark.

"What has you out wandering around?" Coast asked.

"Power blinked a bit ago. Thought I better check on the generator. Filled it up in case the power goes out for real. When I saw you pull in, I wanted to let you know about the power and that I checked your generator, too. Didn't know how late you would be out."

"Appreciate it, brother."

"Do you lose power out this way often?" Mackenzie asked as she looked around. The only lights that could be seen were through the windows of the others' homes and several strategically placed outdoor lights we had mounted around the property. Even then, it was still dark, and when the trees swayed from the wind, they cast eerie shadows. Sometimes it made it look as if people were darting from tree to tree.

"Not too often, but when it goes out, sometimes it takes the power company a while to get around to us since we're outside of town. A generator pumps enough power to keep the fridge running and a light or two on," Coast answered Mackenzie's question.

"I bet it's spooky out here when there are no lights on at all."

Mackenzie was right. It was. At least it had been to me and the others when we were growing up. Because even with houses and the clubhouse on the compound, most of the land around the area was woods. It hadn't helped that six young boys enjoyed using the darkness to scare the shit out of each other and anyone else who was around.

"It can be," Coast said, then chuckled. "The club hasn't always had the generators, though. Our dads talked about getting them, but they kept putting off buying them since we seldom lose power. Devil was the reason they finally equipped each house and the clubhouse with them."

I grinned. "Shit, what were we? Seven or eight. Damn, if I close my eyes and think about it, I swear I can still feel the burn on my ass from the spanking my dad gave me," I said as I recalled one of the many times we had gotten into trouble while growing up. My brothers and I were continuously sitting in Stroker's office, facing him and the other dads for one or a half dozen reasons.

"Hell, brother, I not only received a spanking from my dad. That was the day I learned every curse word in the Spanish language."

Mackenzie looked between us, then asked, "Are one of you going to tell me what Devil did to cause all of you to get in trouble?"

Coast smiled down at Mackenzie. Even in the limited light, I could read his facial expression. The man was a goner over Mac. He had chased her long enough. I was happy for him.

I tuned back into the story Coast was telling, "…the wind took out the power, leaving the whole compound pitch black. You couldn't even see the moon and stars for the clouds. Shakes, Dare's ol' lady, was watching us at their house while the dads, Dare, Roscoe, Payton, along with a few members and a couple prospects who lived on the compound then, started filling coolers with ice, making sure everyone's cabin and the clubhouse had enough wood for the fireplaces after the power had been out for a couple of hours. Shakes had their fireplace going, and we were in the living room playing games on the floor by the light from the fire and candles she had spread through the room. Shakes was curled up on the couch watching us, and then she fell asleep."

I grinned the whole time Coast talked while Mackenzie was glued to every word he said. The story brought back so many memories of my brothers. It even surprised me I hadn't remembered the story when I found the dead raccoon underneath my dad's place.

Coast continued, leaving out no details. By Mackenzie's facial expressions, she was enjoying every word. Hell, I was too, if I was being honest.

By the time he got to the end of the story where Shakes had woken up with the bear's face staring at her, and how her scream, then our screams scared the raccoons. Which caused them to take off through the house, then the front door flying open and banging off the wall as the dads and Dare busted in with guns drawn—Coast and I were both laughing.

Mackenzie laughed, too, then shook her head. "Oh my God, every one of you deserved to get spanked," she said and looked at us.

I chuckled, then added. "The dads and Dare spent two hours with flashlights trying to find where the raccoons had run off to. Christ, they were mad as hell."

I noticed Mackenzie shiver; the temperature dropping since it had gotten dark. Coast saw her reaction, too. "Let's get you in the house and off your feet, *cariño*. I promised you dinner," he said and started leading Mackenzie toward his house. I walked with them across the yard, headed toward my place.

"Enjoy your dinner, brother," I called out as Coast turned them toward the door while I continued to my place. I was happy for my brother; I knew he and Mackenzie would work out. Coast had finally gone after what he wanted most. But even though I was happy for him, I felt a little forlorn. I wanted to find the same connection with a woman as each of my brothers had found.

I had only taken a few steps when it hit me what I had said to Mackenzie after lunch at the diner when Coast had been out of town at his great grandfather's place on the reservation. She had thought no one noticed her looking around for Coast that day. But I had. When I told her where Coast was, she had acted like she hadn't cared. I informed her she would know when he got back into town because he would come for her. I had been right, too. "Mackenzie?"

"Yes," she replied as she looked over her shoulder.

"Told you," I said and continued walking toward my house.

"Told me, what?" Mackenzie questioned.

"He'd come looking for you," I said, reminding her, and then smiled when there was no response from her, but from Coast.

"By the way, brother, me and you need to have a talk."

My smile widened, and I chuckled. "Sure, man. Can you wait and thank me later? I'm heading to Whispering Nights."

"Weren't you considering dropping your membership?" Coast asked.

I had forgotten I mentioned it to him the last time he and I had sat on his porch drinking a beer after we had finished at the garage. It had been before Jag and River married.

"Yeah, but recently I came across a reason to postpone my decision. At least for the time being."

"Good for you. Who knows, maybe this reason will be the one," Coast said.

If my brother only knew the stuff that had been going through my head earlier about Gabriella, he would never let me live it down. None of my brothers would.

"Not sure, though I'm enjoying finding out." At least tonight I would be, but Coast didn't need to know any details. Especially that I had only met Gabriella a couple weeks ago, and we hadn't gotten any further than me showing her around the club.

When she and I finished the tour, I led her to the sitting area off to the side of the main floor. We needed to talk and get comfortable with each other if anything was going happened between us, which I hoped for.

I had looked forward to learning everything about her, which was a first for me. Usually, I jumped right into the discussion of limits and what a sub expected from her Dom and what I would expect from her. However, Gabriella had received a text and apologized for having to cut our time short, but she needed to leave.

Only after I witnessed the genuine regret flash in her eyes as she glanced around the club had I pushed for a set time we would meet and try again. Another first for me, setting up a preset time for an encounter with a submissive. Hell, I seldom repeated with a sub, and on the occasion I did, the time between encounters reached months. Somehow, I had known as I watched her taillights disappear into the night when she pulled out of the parking lot that Gabriella would change my life.

Hadn't she already started after only being around her for a couple of hours at the most?

"I bet you are. Be safe, brother," Coast's voice brought me back to the present because once again, I allowed Gabriella into my head. It seemed to happen regularly.

"Always," I replied to Coast, then turned toward my house and entered instead of going to my truck. Talking with Coast and Mackenzie had settled the anxiousness I had previously felt. I even wondered if it was all about Gabriella or was it my subconscious trying to alert me that my guarded control was slipping?

I grabbed a bottle of water from my fridge and sat down at the island in my kitchen. I closed my eyes and reached for the control I needed as much as the air I breathed. When it settled through me and I felt it snap firmly in place, I opened my eyes, rose from my seat, and tossed the plastic bottle into the trash before I walked back out the door.

Not once in my entire life had I let a woman have influence over my emotions or how I lived my life. A few hours with Gabriella would not change that. At least it was what I repeated to myself as I pulled out onto the main road and steered my truck toward Whispering Nights. I was confident the evening would be like any other at the club.

Gabriella would prove me wrong.

Chapter Two

Gabriella

"Mom! Can I take the Frozen DVD to Mrs. Grissom's? She hasn't seen the movie."

I placed the last plate in the dishwasher and closed it before I answered Sawyer, "Are you sure she wants to watch it?"

"Yes. She told me the next time I stayed to bring it, and we would make popcorn and watch it. So… can I?" Sawyer asked, this time from the doorway that separated the family room from the kitchen. DVD in her hand.

"Sure, set it with your backpack, so we don't forget it." I dried my hands with the dishtowel, then folded it and laid it beside the sink.

"Can I take the bag of M&M's and the Clue game, too?"

I thought of what happened the last time she took a whole mega bag of M&M's to Eleanor's house. "How about just the game? We don't want a repeat of what happened the last time, do we?"

"Nope, it was gross. But if I promise not to eat the entire bag after Mrs. Grissom falls asleep, can I take the bag? I promise not to text even if I barf."

My daughter was an excellent negotiator for her age. Or maybe just relentless when she wanted her way.

"Game, no candy."

"Are you saying no because you had to leave your date last time?"

Her question brought a reminder of where I was planning to spend the evening, along with the butterflies in my stomach, which always appeared when I thought of Max. He liked having his first name used where I had noticed most of the men in the club used either Mister with their surname or Master with or without the first name attached. Though I already knew when we got down to business, so to speak, I was to answer with 'Yes Sir or No Sir.' There were no exceptions.

Joining Whispering Nights might have been viewed by others as a rash decision made from reading too many romance books. In actuality, I had found I had a lot in common with the submissives between the pages of the books I read. Enough so that I researched everything I could find on D/s relationships. The more I uncovered, the more my interest piqued. To hand over sexual control to another individual whose knowledge would bring you pleasure and enhance their pleasure was definitely worth the effort. And though I had only spent a limited time around Max, I had felt comfortable, even safe with him. Two things I hadn't felt around any man since Justin, and even with him, it had taken time being together for the feelings to surface.

"Mom! Mom!"

"Huh?" I absently asked and looked down at Sawyer with her eyebrows scrunched as she looked at me.

"Are you okay? Your cheeks are red. Why were you staring at the ceiling, anyway? Are you going to answer my question?"

I shook my head and smiled. "Don't you tire of asking so many questions, Sawyer?"

"Nope. How am I 'posed to learn anything if I don't ask? Nonno says the more you know, the fewer people can screw over you."

I pinched the bridge of my nose, took a deep breath, and then blew it out before I replied to my daughter. My dad, Nero Agassi, hanged the moon as far as his granddaughter was concerned. You would think his words were gospel. "Sawyer, I told you we don't repeat the things your nonno says."

"I know because Nonno uses bad words when he talks, and repeating the words isn't nice or ladylike and will get me into trouble. Maybe I can start making him and Zio Enzo pay me when they say bad words in front of me like Ally does her zios and nonnos?"

I couldn't help but smile at the fact Sawyer, who had questions for everything imaginable, found nothing out of the ordinary with her newest, *bestest* friend's multitude of aunts, uncles, and grandpas. Then again, Sawyer had lived around her own group of *aunts* and *uncles* between the Agassi and Tanucci sides of our family. It was probably why she and I felt comfortable around the men and women of the Black Hawk MC. From what I had witnessed, the MC dynamics weren't much different from what we were used to with our Italian family. Once accepted into the fold, there was nothing either of them wouldn't do for you. However, break the trust and loyalty given—and the cost would most likely result in more than anyone wanted or was willing to pay.

"They pay Ally, huh?" When I thought of little Ally collecting money from the big bikers, it took everything not to laugh.

"Yep. Her mom makes her put most of the money in the bank. She's 'posed to use it for college."

"I'll tell you what. When we are around the family at Thanksgiving, if you can get your nonno and zio or the others to fork cash over to you, it is all yours, baby girl."

"Yes! And at Christmas, too? Plus, I didn't think of my other zias and zios," she said and pumped her fist.

I chuckled. "Hey, if you are successful in getting anyone in the family to pay up, Zio Marco may offer you a job." It was out of mouth without thought.

"Wow, do you think he would let me be in charge of all the dollars in his casinos?"

There was no way to explain the Tanucci side of our family. Sawyer had years before she learned their activities in Las Vegas extended to more than owning and running a couple of casinos. She'd also learn it was easy and in your best interest to turn your head to some of their dealings. After all, whether right or wrong, they were family.

"Maybe." It was time for me to change the subject. "While I go change, why don't you go to your room and put on your pajamas? That way, when I get home tonight and pick you up from Eleanor's, you'll be ready for bed."

"Okay." Sawyer turned and ran across the family room and placed the DVD in her backpack. As I started down the hallway that led to the bedrooms, Sawyer was quick to catch up to me. "Is your date with Dr. Booger?"

"No, and his name isn't Booger, Sawyer. It's Booker. Dr. Booker."

Sawyer stopped at her bedroom door. "That's not what you called him on the phone with Zia Tori."

My lips twitched as I fought to keep from laughing. I would have to watch what I said while talking with my sister when Sawyer was present. "I think you need to go change before my ears bleed."

"You always say that when you don't want to answer me," Sawyer said. Her face showing the unhappiness of not getting answers to her questions.

"Well, there you go. Now go change. I won't be too long."

Sawyer walked into her room, and I turned toward mine. At least dealing with my daughter had temporarily taken my mind off the evening ahead and calmed the butterflies in my stomach.

Once I was showered and dressed, Sawyer, with backpack in hand, and I walked next door to Eleanor's house.

I had lucked out in the neighbor department when Sawyer and I moved into the rancher I rented upon moving to the area. Mrs. Grissom had turned out to be a lifesaver for a mother and daughter moving to a new town. I had worried about finding someone trustworthy to watch Sawyer while I worked to build my pediatric practice.

When Eleanor had volunteered to care for Sawyer, it had felt as if an enormous weight lifted off my shoulders. Not only didn't I have to worry about my daughter while I worked, but Eleanor had also volunteered to continue watching her when she started school. I jumped all over it. Eleanor had informed me that being widowed and living alone, Sawyer's company was a welcomed change to her otherwise quiet and boring days. She and Mr. Grissom hadn't had any children, and though she had two younger sisters, they lived on the east coast. I wondered why she hadn't moved to be near them after her husband had passed, but I hadn't wanted to pry to fill my curiosity. If she wanted me to know, she would have mentioned it.

With Sawyer settled at Mrs. Grissom's house, I headed back to my house to grab my keys and purse. Double-checking the doors were secured before I went out into the garage to my car. The butterflies reappeared in my stomach as I left the town limits and made my way toward Whispering Nights... and ultimately... Max.

Chapter Three

Flirt

Even knowing I was early I started scanning the area as soon as I stepped through the main door and into Whispering Nights.

"Looking for anyone in particular, Max?" was asked behind me, followed by a chuckle.

I turned. "You know, I liked it better when Stella was here to keep you occupied. You weren't left with time to harass me or the others."

"Ha! See how much attention you pay? I don't harass the others in the club. I save it up for when I see you, my friend." Mark stuck his hand out, and taking it with mine, we shook hands.

"Don't I feel special," I said as we walked further into the club. We reached an area out of the way of the other members but could still see the entrance and everything else going on in the club on the main floor.

"You should. Not everyone gets my vast knowledge shared with them."

"You're in a good mood. Stella must be around. Where is she? In your office?" I asked and with my eyes swept the area looking for Mark's wife, which was a sign I wasn't thinking correctly. If Stella was in the club and not in Mark's office, she would have been by his side. No submissive in a D/s relationship would be running loose in the club, they could only be in certain sections of the club.

"Not tonight. Tomorrow will be her first time back at the club since having Chrissy. She finally found a babysitter she trusts for longer than a trip to the grocery store. The young woman is scheduled to watch Chrissy tomorrow night. I must admit I haven't been this excited since... well, I can't remember," Mark said and laughed at himself.

"You're finally getting your sub back, man. You have the right to be excited."

"It's more than that, Max. I'm getting my wife back. Don't get me wrong, I love my little girl and wouldn't trade having her for anything, but I've missed my wife. It's been a learning experience on how to multitask being parents to Chrissy without losing us as a couple."

"If my brothers can do it, I'm sure you can, too."

"If you said that months ago, I'm not sure I would have agreed. But I think Stella and I have finally started getting the parents' thing down."

"One day, I would love to face the same problems," I said and meant it more than I thought I ever would.

"Hey, who knows, maybe *she'll* be what you're looking for," Mark said, and I followed where he was looking.

Gabriella stood inside the entrance as if anyone made the wrong move, she would bolt. Not a chance I was going to let that happen.

"Coast said almost the same to me earlier," I answered and took a step in Gabriella's direction with Mark following beside me.

"Then you should listen. Two of us cannot be wrong. I'm just sorry I didn't get the chance to grill you on how the tour went. However, after you walked her out, you never made it back inside the club."

"There is nothing to grill me about. She received a text and had to leave. I set a time up with her for us to meet tonight, and here she is. I'm sure there is someone else you could or need to check in with. Don't let me keep you," I said as we walked across the room, and I kept my eyes on Gabriella. Out of my peripheral vision I noticed several of the Doms scattered around the area had their eyes focused on Gabriella, too.

Mark snorted. "I think I'll say hello to Gabriella, if you don't mind? Considering this is my club and all."

"By all means… just don't stick around."

"Hmm… that response is interesting. Especially coming from you." I heard the humor in Mark's voice, and it annoyed me. His response was meant to goad me, and even though I knew it—it was working.

"You're trying to be a dick and reading too much into this."

"Am I?" Mark replied as we reached Gabriella, leaving me with no time to respond.

"Hi," Gabriella said, and I cocked a brow but didn't respond to her greeting.

"Evening, Gabriella," Mark replied, then gave her a chance to correct her mistake before he brough it to her attention. "You seem to have forgotten you are inside the walls of Whispering Nights."

My lips twitched at the dumbfounded look she graced Mark with. Then I quickly sobered, remembered she was new to the whole BDSM scene. I wondered if her looks alone had drawn me or maybe I wanted to experience what my club brothers had found, and I was the one who read too much into the feelings she caused. When it was only an attraction to a beautiful woman.

Her expression changed, and I knew her mistake in greeting us had finally registered with her. "Umm... sorry. Let me try that again. Hello, Master Mark, Master Max."

"Glad to know a few of the rules stuck we discussed in our short time together," I said, and if I hadn't watched her so closely, I would have missed the slight narrowing of her eyes before they went back to normal.

"Yes, Sir," she paused, then added. "I'm a very fast learner."

As I stared at Gabriella and struggled to keep my stoic composure to *Sir* rolling out in her throaty voice, I almost missed Mark's attempt to cover a chuckle with a cough.

"I guess I'll be on my way and leave you both to it," he commented, then slapped me on the shoulder, causing me to break eye contact with her and glance toward him.

"Why don't you do that. We can catch you later," I said.

Mark smirked as he replied, "Count on it, my friend," then turned his head and added. "Gabriella," with a nod before he walked away toward his office without waiting for her to respond.

"Go to the ladies' room and put your jacket and purse in a locker." I had shown her where the room was when we had taken the tour. Not only was it a restroom. It was equipped with showers and lockers with locks that could be reset to any combination the user chose. Even the lockers assigned to individuals permanently to store anything they didn't want to carry back and forth from their homes every time they came to the club. There was also the same setup in the men's locker room at the other end of the hall. "I'll grab a couple of bottles of water from the bar and wait for you to return. Meet me there."

"Yes… Sir."

I waited until she walked away before I grinned at her close call to address me. Pleased she had caught herself.

By the time I went to the bar, held the water bottles in my hand and asked Mitch, one of the floor monitors to do me a favor, Gabriella returned.

"Any problems?" I asked as I handed Mitch my jacket and the key to my personal locker in the men's room. I could have gone at the same time as Gabriella, but I wanted to see how she reacted to orders, and I admit I was a tad shocked she hadn't bulked in the least. Mitch would place my bag in one of the private rooms, guaranteeing one would be empty when we were ready to play. Because if I read Gabriella right, no way was she ready for the open play area on the main floor. Only time would tell if she ever would be.

"No, Sir."

"No hesitation this time. Very good. Now let's go to the sitting area and have a talk, shall we?" I held both bottles of water in one hand and waved the empty hand out toward the sitting area. As we walked, I kept very little space between us. Just enough where we didn't brush against each other. However, when we reached an empty couch, I waited for her to sit. After I set the two bottles on the table in front of us, I sat next to her, purposely invading her space. It was something I would do a lot more of before the night was over.

Chapter Four

Gabriella

When I walked through the entrance of the club, there had been no need to look around to know eyes were locked onto me—I felt them. It took every ounce of my strength not to turn around and leave. Eventually I mustered enough courage and scanned the area to look for Max. I had no clue what I would have done if I hadn't spotted him across the room. He stood with Master Mark talking, then his head turned and he looked directly at me.

I hadn't been thinking when I joined a BDSM club. I knew nothing about any of it outside of what I had read. Between the romances with BDSM elements and some articles I found through the search engine on the net, it still left me with just the basic information.

If I had half of a brain, I would have left, called Master Mark tomorrow and apologize and explain I had made a mistake.

Instead, I stood there, debated in my head whether or not I had lost my mind, and watched as both men walked toward me. Why did the man have to look so dang good? Everything was his fault. He was tall, blond, and there were models who would never look as good as Max in a pair of black jeans, a black t-shirt, and a leather jacket that showed more than just a little wear and tear. So yes, the blame rested at his feet.

Max moved like a man who was confident and comfortable in his skin. His body language alone screamed dominant alpha male.

As he and Master Mark approached, they were talking, but I had no clue what was being said. I was too focused on Max's piercing brown eyes directed at me. When I finally regained my speech ability and acknowledged the two men, I had forgotten the most basic rule of a submissive addressing a Dom or Master.

Thanks to Master Mark's polite reminder, it registered and then I corrected my blunder. Master Mark seemed satisfied. Max not so much. His statement about 'Glad something stuck' blah blah blah, irked me enough to settle my previous 'take flight' nervousness and replace it with annoyance.

I didn't understand how one man in minutes made me go through several emotions.

When Max sat down next to me on the couch, to the point we were almost touching but not, I wasn't sure if I wanted to laugh or cry. I knew it was a strategic move and the knowledge of it hadn't kept the slight shiver that coursed through my body from happening. No, the man had barely touched me since we had met, yet he had my system going nuts.

He placed his arm around my shoulders, pulled me closer to him, and the sliver of space between us dissolved. He lifted his hand off my shoulder and weaved his fingers through my hair until the tips of them brushed the skin on the back of my neck.

"Do I make you nervous?"

"No, Sir," I quickly responded. Too quickly.

Max's hand moved and until his whole hand rest against my neck. Leaning down, he put his mouth to my ear and said, "Don't lie to me," as he squeezed my neck.

I took a deep breath and blew it out. "Okay, maybe a little," I acknowledged. Shocked at how the words came out breathy even after I had taken the cleansing breath. I wasn't sure I liked the effect the man had on me.

Max shifted, turned his body more toward me, then reached out with his other arm and laid his hand just above my knee.

"Just a little?" he asked before he leaned his head closer, then sucked my earlobe into his mouth as his hand caressed its way up my thigh and back down while the hand on my neck held me in place.

The small moan that escaped caught me off guard. Still, before I had the time to become embarrassed over being in the open, he bit down on my earlobe, then released it and ran his tongue down my neck. His hand he had slid to the inside of my thigh made the journey upward.

The beat of my heart sped up, my eyes closed, and I tilted my head to the side to give him better access. Unconsciously I widened my legs, which gave his hand an uninterrupted path to my core that was quickly beginning to heat.

"Here is the key to your locker and the one to room seven. Everything is ready for you," was said in a voice laced with amusement. My eyes snapped open, and the man Max had spoken with at the bar stood in front of us.

Max straightened, dropped his hand from my neck, and pulled the other from between my legs. As he did, his hand brushed against the seam of my pants at my center. I bit down on my tongue to keep the moan from escaping, but could do nothing to halt my body's reaction.

"Thanks, Mitch," Max said as he took the keys Mitch held out.

"Anytime," he answered, then turned his head in my direction and ran his eyes over me before looking back to Max and adding. "This is the first time I'm actually disappointed that you do not allow viewing." Max grinned, and Mitch gave me one last look before he walked away.

I had a pretty good idea what Mitch meant about viewing. Which wasn't going to work for me. No way I wanted to be on display. Max had shown me the private room area and several of them had windows with shades that could be opened if the occupants wished to allow people to stop and watch. I let out an unladylike snort thinking of them.

"Is there a problem?"

"I just thought if store windows had the same type of displays rooms the club has, they would have plenty of customer traffic going past."

Max smiled and held out his hand. I placed my hand in his, and he pulled me to my feet. "No doubt they would, but their aim is to get the customers in the store. Not gathering on the sidewalk outside."

"True," I answered as he bent and grabbed our forgotten bottles of water between the fingers of his free hand. We walked in the direction that would lead us to the hallway where the private rooms were located. I expected the nervousness to rear its ugly head and was shocked when it didn't. I wasn't sure how one man could keep me calm and stir me up at the same time.

When we reached the door, he let go of the hand he was holding to use one of the keys Mitch had given him. He unlocked the door and turned the knob, pushing it open, then placed a hand at the small of my back and led me in. I noticed every time he touched me, warmth flooded my system. He didn't even have to directly connect with my skin for me to experience it. What was more disconcerting to me was being around him—a total of two times—felt like coming home.

How in the hell was that even possible?

Chapter Five

Flirt

"Gabriella?" I said to draw her attention when she had stopped in her tracks after leading her into the room. After touching her and running my lips against her skin while on the couch, I could have continued and taken her right there. I had purposely set out to push her to see if she had an ounce of submissive in her, and it had backfired on me. In the years of going to clubs, I never had an immediate connection to a submissive as I was experiencing with her. Hell, I never had an immediate connection to any woman, period, in or out of a club.

Not to say I wasn't attracted on a physical level to other women, just not to where I struggled with my constraint. Nor had I experienced the need to be what they desired outside of our time in the club. With Gabriella, the need to swoop her up and lock her away in my home was a craving I wanted to indulge in. The knowledge didn't sit well.

To be afraid wasn't or has never been in my genetic makeup, but I found myself worried that once I had all of her—the fear she wouldn't feel the same laid under the surface mocking me. How many times had I said to my brothers that if I found the woman for me, I would do whatever it took, even if it meant tying her to my bed? I wasn't ready to answer the question.

"Gabriella? Are you okay?" I asked again and watched her body jolt.

"Ah… yes… sorry. My mind had gone somewhere else for a second," she said, and the blush that formed on her cheeks made me wonder what had distracted her. I held off asking and focused on the fact she hadn't answered correctly. It was time I started treating her as the submissive she seemed to think she was.

Mark was diligent in vetting the people he allowed in his club. Yet I wasn't a hundred percent Gabriella was the submissive he signed up.

Who reads erotica romance books and thinks 'yes, that is me' and runs out and joins a BDSM club?

"Have you forgotten how to address me properly? Or how you are to address any Master, Dom, or Domme when you are inside this club?" I asked in a firmer voice as I watched closely and waited for her response. Her eyes narrowed, then just as quickly as though she realized what she was doing, she dropped her eyes.

"Sorry for the lapse. It won't happen again, Sir," she replied, keeping her eyes cast downward.

"Very good, Angel," I praised and moved to stand in front of her. "Hopefully, you won't have to be reminded again. Not all Doms are as understanding as I am, and you would earn punishments for anything they deemed disrespectful. Do you understand?"

"Yes, Sir."

"Excellent." I walked to one of the two chairs in the room where Mitch had set my bag on the floor. All rooms were set up to accommodate almost every scenario, to include if a sub had more than one Dom. I sat the two bottles of water I held in my hand on the table that separated the two chairs.

Gabriella stayed in the same spot, though I noticed she watched me through her eyelashes.

I squatted by the bag, unzipped it, and then looked inside to make sure I had everything I planned to introduce her to. Every item in my bag had either been sanitized or purchased new. I pulled several things out and placed them on the seat of the chair while I reached back in and pulled out a couple of condoms and a tube of lube.

I caught movement out of the corner of my eye and turned my head toward her. The hands which had been by her sides were in front of her clasped together. Her body language defying her previous calm.

I picked up the items from the chair, then walked to where the bench sat in front of the window. I placed my items on top of a stand between the bench and the swing that was in the corner.

"Max, I mean… Sir, are you going to close the shade?" I could hear the trepidation in her voice.

I hit the button beside the window, the blind inside the glass descended. By the time I made my way to the chair and sat, the blind was down, closing the outside world out.

"Come here, Gabriella." I pointed to the spot in front of me.

I watched her chest rise and fall as she took a deep breath, then let it out. She turned and began taking languid steps toward me. Her facial expression was blank, but her eyes showed determination. So much so, it surprised me her chin wasn't lifted in challenge.

"What is your safe word?" I asked as she stopped in front of me.

"Red, Sir."

"And if you use your safe word?"

"Everything stops, Sir."

I grabbed the sides of my t-shirt, pulling it free from the waist of my jeans, and her eyes followed as I raised it, reached over my shoulders and yanked it over my head. Once I had removed it, I tossed it over the arm of the extra chair, then leaned back.

The tip of Gabriella's tongue peeked out of her mouth and licked across her lips. Pure willpower was the only thing that kept me from going instantly hard. And I would swear the movement of her eyes over my bare chest sent scorching heat through my system. The woman who stood before me was dangerous to my being, and she had no clue. Any nervousness or uncertainty she had previously was gone.

For the very first time since I had walked into any club, the appeal of having a submissive of my own pushed forward. The picture of Gabriella down on her knees, her hands cuffed behind her, my cock sliding over her tongue was only one scene flashing through my head. I pictured a hundred things to do with her, and with each one, I hardened to the point I shifted to ease some of the discomfort. So much for the control over my body.

"Strip," I ordered, causing her eyes to snap back to mine and off my chest. She blinked, and I waited for her to balk. Instead, she astounded me when without a word she bent at the waist and reached for the zipper on the back of her knee-high boots. The room was so quiet I could hear the teeth on the zipper giving way. She placed a hand on the arm of my chair, bent her leg and grabbed the back of the heel, pulling the boot off. It hit the floor, and she repeated the same process with the other boot.

Gabriella straightened and reached around to her back. I heard another zipper, then her hands moved to the sides at the waist and she began pushing her tight leather pants down. Once they were over her hips and made it to her thighs, I got the first glimpse of the tiny patch of red lace that was doing a terrible job at covering her mound. A bare mound.

She finished removing her pants and tossed them into the seat of the chair beside me, then moved her fingers to the buttons of the shirt. The dark blue material fitted to her frame, and as the first two buttons released, a flash of red was exposed. The front parted, and the matching red bra to her panties came into view along with full breasts barely contained in the lacy material. She pitched the shirt on top of the pants before reaching for the clasp of her bra.

"Leave those." I hardly recognized my voice for the hoarseness. I leaned forward, reached my arm out, and used my knuckles to touch the exposed part of her breasts. Her skin was soft and smooth, and I couldn't wait to glide my tongue over every inch.

Wrapping her wrists with my hands, I held her in place and moved closer until my nose bumped against the area above the red lace thong. My tongue snaked out, the tip connecting with her skin. I slid my tongue from right to left and paused when I hit a difference in her skin's texture at her hipbone. There were tiny lines, narrow and faded enough that no one would notice them unless they were as close as I was. The stretch marks showed Gabriella had at least one child.

I moved my tongue to the center and licked a path up the center until I reached her bellybutton and circled it. The small taste of her made me hold a groan back. I released her wrists and placed my hands on her hips, pulling her closer. Sliding my hands down her hips, enjoying her curves as I moved my hands behind her, running my palms over the globes of her ass. I pushed a finger under the string of her

55

thong and followed it down the crease until I reached the puckered entrance. Pushing the finger against the hole, testing its resistance. Easing off only to press harder when I brought the finger back.

Gabriella shivered, and her breathing picked up. "You like that, Angel?" I pushed a little harder until the tip barely spread the opening.

"Yes." I slapped the cheek of her ass. "Sir," she added quickly.

"Damn, we are definitely going to explore anal. Just not right now. I imagine your tight little hole is going to strangle my cock, Angel. Thinking about is making me hard." I removed my finger and slid it from under the string, and with a quick squeeze of the cheek of her ass, I moved to the thin elastic at her hips. I latched on, sliding the thong down. When the lace reached the floor, she stepped out of them, and then I reached for the clasp on the front of her bra and freed her breasts. I tossed the bra toward the chair, leaned in and placed my mouth on one of her breasts.

I circled my tongue around the outer edge of the rosy areola. Sucked the peaked nipple between my lips and bit gently down while I massaged the other with my hand. Stopping only to tweak its nipple. Giving it attention while I enjoyed teasing the other with my mouth.

Gabriella reached out and clutched my shoulders, her nails pressing down on the skin. It was the first time she had touched me since we entered the room, and later I wouldn't be surprised to find moon-shaped indents in my skin.

I thought to scold her for touching me without permission, but then she wiggled her hips, moaned, and dug her nails deeper into my skin. She would be my downfall and at that moment I didn't a shit.

I released her nipple with a pop. "You need my mouth somewhere else, Angel?" I ran my hand down her body until

56

I reached the gap between her legs. I pushed two fingers through the gap, using them to part her pussy lips and sliding them through, coating them with her wet heat.

"Oh God, please," she said with a moan and pressed down, shifting her hips trying to ride my fingers.

I stood abruptly, placed my other hand on her backside to hold her in place. "Spread your legs wider." She immediately obeyed, and I pushed both fingers inside her core.

Gabriella's forehead landed on my chest, and she rocked her hips. Pushing down and forcing my fingers deeper.

I rotated my hand and twisted my fingers as I moved them in and out. As her legs trembled, I knew she was close to climaxing. I pulled my fingers out, and she whimpered. We locked eyes when she raised her head, and I lifted my hand and stuck the fingers in my mouth and sucked. Her taste exploded on my tongue, and my cock jumped. The need to lay her out on the bench and pound into her was so intense I had to take several deep breaths to settle my system. It was supposed to be her first experience, and I was essentially the guide on her journey. But fuck me if I wasn't ready to feel her wrapped around my cock.

Taking hold of her arm, I headed toward the bench, then stopped and moved to the swing. Once I had her positioned with her back supported and her neck resting against the pillow, I lifted her legs one at a time and placed them in the stirrups.

"Raise your arms so I can adjust the hand straps." When she was ready, I turned and grabbed the flogger off the table. Gabriella watched my every move, saying nothing. "Doing okay, Angel?"

"Yes... Sir."

"Are you upset I didn't let you come before?" Silence greeted my question. My lips twitched as I looked into her very expressive eyes. "I asked a question, Angel. I expect an answer. Maybe you would prefer to use your safe word and put a stop to everything."

Christ, I was pushing her. If she used her safe word, I would stop, though I wanted anything but to.

"Yes! Sir." Her response was a slap to my system.

"Then say the word, Gabriella, and we will call it a night."

"I don't want to use my safe word, Sir," she said as she tried to adjust herself on the swing by pulling on the hand straps.

"So you were upset I didn't let you come?" I slapped the leather strips of the flogger across the palm of my hand.

"Yes, Sir."

I took a deep breath. "Angel, I didn't want you to come right then," I explained—which was a first for me—and stepped between her spread legs. "When you come, it's going to be with my cock buried deep inside you." I grazed the leather tails of the flogger over her pussy.

"Oh, Sir," was all she said while her eyes flashed with heat, and she wiggled in the swing.

I ran the soft leather tails up over her stomach, and when I reached the middle of her breasts, I slid them over one, then the other. The snap of my wrist had the tails tapping her breast hard enough to cause a slight sting. I alternated, tapping each a few times. Her nipples hardened from the attention and faint red marks formed on her gold skin. I glided the leather back over her body and without pause slapped the leather tails on the inside of her thighs. Alternating from one to the other, bringing the tails close enough to her center that she would feel the small whoosh of air against her mound.

She moaned and arched her back. I repeatedly went over her body. Soft touches, then hard. Gabriella's moans grew louder with each pass, her pussy shined with her juices. My cock was rock hard and pressed painfully against the zipper of my jeans.

"You still with me, Angel?" I asked as I stepped back. Her eyes focused on me filled with desire. I tossed the flogger on the table and grabbed a foil package I had set out, stuffing the condom into my pocket. To relieve some of my discomfort, I unfastened my belt and my pants.

"Please, Sir," she said, followed by a moan. Her response causing the small amount of control I had left, evaporate.

Pulling my cock free as I turned back to Gabriella, the weight of my erection bobbed in her direction as I moved back between her legs. I placed my arms under her thighs, putting the swing into motion. Bringing her center to my mouth, then using my tongue, I licked from back to front, tasting her essence as it exploded on my tongue.

I slid my tongue through her folds and reached her clit. Circling it before sucking the hardening nub between my lips. She tried to raise her hips; the swing moving with her action. I tightened my hold on her, keeping her and the swing where I wanted them as I continued my mouth's and tongue's assault on her pussy.

The shiver ran through her body when I pierced my tongue through her slit and into her opening. I fucked her with my tongue until her head flew back, her body shook, and my name came from between her lips.

When she came down from her orgasm, I pulled my tongue away, released her legs, and retrieved the condom from my pocket. After pushing my jeans down, I made quick work of the wrapper and rolled the condom on.

I pumped my cock twice, then centered it at her opening. Placing a hand on each hip, I pulled her toward me until I buried myself inside her.

Gabriella's body bowed, and she held onto the straps so tightly her knuckles whitened.

"Doing okay, Angel? Do you need your safe word?" I asked and took a second to work on my control while I waited for her to respond. I hoped when she did, it wasn't with her safe word. If she did, I would have no one to blame but myself. I lost focus on what I was supposed to be doing. She was the novice, and I was to introduce her to the aspects of BDSM. Though I had started out that way—I hadn't followed through. Gabriella threatened the control I was known for.

With her walls wrapped tight around and the heat radiating through, I gritted my teeth to keep from shooting off as if it were my very first time.

"No, please. I need you to move, Sir. Please."

Christ, the plea from her snapped my constraint, and I withdrew and pushed back in. I used the swing's momentum, pushing it away and pulling it forward along with the thrust of my hips. The rhythm stayed the same, but I picked up the pace until the muscles in my arms burned.

The familiar tingle started in my spine, moved to tighten my balls, and the pressure built, readying for the explosion.

Gabriella arched her back, and when her walls began to spasm around me, my orgasm released, and I filled the condom.

As I stood there, buried deep inside Gabriella—while we both fought for breath—the realization she was what I was searching for struck me deep in my core.

She was everything I had been waiting on.

Chapter Six

Gabriella

I sat across Max's lap with my head on his shoulder while he rubbed his hand up and down my arm and had no memory of either of us getting dressed. I briefly wondered if saying 'thank you' would be inappropriate under the circumstances. Or would it be over the top to ask for his address and send him a thank you gift? What would a woman even buy a man for giving her mind-blowing orgasms?

For all I knew we could have been sitting for minutes or hours. His heartbeat was steady and the sound of it soothing. I was an experienced woman as far as sex was concerned. At least I thought so before Max. A slight shiver went through my body as I thought of the first contact of the flogger and the slight sting, which quickly turned into pleasure. How was it possible that a man I recently met knew more about my sexual need than I did?

"Are you cold, Angel?" Max asked and continued rubbing my arm along with placing his other hand on my leg and duplicating the process.

"A little," I lied, not wanting to admit the real reason. As an afterthought, I added, "Sir."

"Ah, Angel, I appreciate the effort," he said, chuckled, and smacked my thigh before removing his hand. He snagged one bottle of water off the side table and handed it to me. "Drink."

I nodded, took the bottle from him, and twisted the cap off. The water was room temperature, yet still soothed my parched throat. Max reached for the other bottle and then brought it toward the hand that had been rubbing my arm. He removed his own cap and drank. After he finished, he set his empty bottle back on the table.

I drank the rest of my water down, then replaced the cap, and shifted on his lap to stand. He clasped my arm and helped me to my feet, then released me.

"Well, I guess we should leave. There could be someone else waiting for the room," I commented, suddenly feeling shy and vulnerable and unable to look at Max's face. Which was stupid, considering everything we had done together.

He reached out and grabbed my hands, holding them in his, and stood. "Are you okay, Gabriella?" His voice soft as he gave my hands a gentle squeeze.

"Yes." It was the only answer I could give him then with so many emotions flooding my system. Once the sexual haze lifted, the onslaught of emotions had taken place. I had gone a long time without letting a man bust through the barriers I had built to protect not only myself but Sawyer, too.

I had loved, and I had lost. Sex was to be an escape from my daily life, nothing more, nothing less. It was why I joined Whispering Nights. It was to be a place where I could turn over the sexual power to someone else for a bit without the worry of them wanting anything else from me.

Instead, I found myself the one who wanted more from the man in front of me. If I had had the energy, I would have laughed at how my plan had backfired before it even got off the ground. The unexpected draw to Max had brought home the fact there was a gaping hole in my plan. A roughly six foot two gaping hole.

"Gabriella, I don't think you are telling me the truth. Do you want to discuss what happened here or what caused the sudden change in your demeanor?" Max asked, and I forced myself to look at him. He frowned, and I wondered just how much he could read by looking into my eyes.

I forced a smile and slipped my hands from his. "No, really, all is good. I was just… wondering what time it is. I didn't want to get to my sitter's house too late," I said, broke eye contact with Max, and gathered the two empty water bottles from the table. After a quick glance around the room, I saw the small trash can and walked to it and tossed the bottles in. I noticed Max's bag sat by the door and realized how out of it I must have been to not remember him putting his things away and moving it from in front of the other chair.

"How many children do you have?" he asked as he walked toward me.

"Just one," I answered as I clasped my hands in front of me, feeling awkward and unsure of what to say or do. Fighting to keep from running out the door or, worse, running toward Max. What happened to fulfilling a need for both of us then going our separate ways? Everything I read and researched made it sound so simple. Wasn't it why I joined the club? No commitments. No dinner to sit through after you find no connection with your date. Not enough time to pursue a relationship even if you found a man you liked.

"A boy or a girl?"

"A girl."

Max bent over and picked up his bag and slung the strap over his shoulder. "Ready?" he asked and placed a hand on the small of my back. When the heat of his touch reached through my shirt to my skin, I knew then nothing with Max would be easy.

We walked out of the room and through the club to where the women's and men's restrooms and locker rooms were. I used the facilities, then retrieved my coat and purse from the locker. As I turned to leave, two women entered, and I stepped to the side to give them room. I smiled tentatively at them as they passed.

"Master Max can make you wet with one look," was said by one woman as I walked out of the locker room area. My step faltered, and I slapped my hand against the wall to keep my balance.

"Girl, I would give anything for him to choose me again. I haven't come that hard since I was with him," the other woman said.

"You might as well get that out of your head. He seldom does repeats, and if he does, they are always months apart. I overheard him talking with one of the other masters, and he has no desire to have a permanent sub," the first woman spoke again, and her words struck me hard. I needed to get out of there before they said more. The old saying 'eavesdroppers hear nothing good of themselves' went through my mind as I pushed off the wall.

"Hey, we haven't seen you around here. You must be new." I turned toward the women. "I'm Crista," the blonde said, and I saw her look at my wrist and the band that signified I was new and unattached.

"Hi, I'm Gabriella," I answered and forced a smile.

Crista waved her hand to the redhead beside her. "This is Stephie."

"It's nice to meet you both," I forced out between my lips, then turned around and walked out of the locker room, not waiting for a reply. When I swung the door open, I wasn't even shocked to see Max in the hallway leaning against the wall.

"Ready, Angel?" he asked as he pushed off the wall.

"Yes," I said and shared yet another forced smile. The moment he touched me, and it felt like coming home, I should have walked away and never looked back. I had lived through heartache once, and I knew if I allowed Max in, he would crush my heart. I wasn't willing or able to pay the price a second time.

As we walked back the entrance area of the club, I was aware of everything going on around me, from the people milling about to the couples heading toward the main floor area. The club was at least double in occupancy from when I first arrived.

Max led us to the entrance/exit doors. Neither of us spoke until we were outside. I reached into my purse and pulled out my keys.

"I am not sure what we are supposed to say. Goodnight, see you around or thank you…" I left off there because really, what else was there for me to say after I overheard the women in the locker room.

"Let's start with, where did you park? Then I can walk you to your car and we can set another club date," Max said.

His words caught me off guard, and I wondered how far out he made a second encounter, considering what I overheard. Color me shocked he wanted to have another session with me.

"Okay," was out of my mouth before I had the chance to consider what his request meant. Before I made a fool out of myself by either pumping a fist in the air because he chose me again or crying at my total ineptness with basic club etiquette. Geez, didn't I sound like I just attended a dinner party. A dinner party where I was on the menu. Where in the hell did the intelligent, well-educated, professional woman go? I silently chastised myself for the brief thoughts and pointed in the direction where I was parked. "The white Toyota Highlander."

"Well, that works out. I'm parked in the same row," he said and placed his hand on my lower back. It seemed he was always touching me, even if it was just a brush of his arm when he stood beside me.

"The parking lot wasn't half this full when I arrived." We cut between a row to reach the one where we parked.

"The lot doesn't start to really fill until around ten," he answered, then pointed to a black extended cab truck and added. "That's me."

Two vehicles down and we reached my car, and I hit the key fob to kill the alarm and unlock the doors. Max grabbed the handle before I could and pulled the door open.

"Next Friday or Saturday work for you?" he asked as I tossed my purse inside and grabbed the 'oh shit' bar and boosted myself into the driver's seat. "You need running bars with the built-in step," he added when I plopped down in the seat.

"I have been meaning to get them, but sometimes there aren't enough hours in a day." I placed the key fob down on the center console and pushed the engine start button.

"So, Friday or Saturday?" he repeated.

"Oh, I can't do every week. It wouldn't be fair to my daughter. I could try to do every other week," I answered and expected to hear the same gripes like a few previous men had voiced when I told them I wasn't going to go out every weekend and leave Sawyer with a sitter. Especially since she already spent a good part of her week with one.

"Alright. How about the same time Friday, week after next?" he asked and pulled out his cell. "What's your number?"

I rattled it off without a thought. Shocked when he hadn't given me the 'you have to make time for yourself' speech. Or 'you can't expect us to have a relationship when we only see each other on the weekend' complaint when I would refuse to go out during the week. The few times I had sex—which sadly could be counted on one hand—then got out of bed to leave, they hadn't understood why I couldn't call the sitter and ask if they would keep Sawyer overnight. Then again, this wasn't an actual date. It was a sexual encounter between adults with no commitment or the chance of one. My phone dinged, and I absently reached for it.

"That's me. I texted you my number in case something comes up and you need to reach me. Or by chance you find yourself freed up and want to meet up with me sooner," he said and winked.

Good grief, I was so out of my element with Max. How did he go from dominant sex god to flirty nice guy? I even wondered if I imagined the women who were talking about him as if he was the 'hit it and quit it' type.

"Um… okay, I will. I guess I'll see you week after next," I said, and when I would have reached for the handle to pull the door closed, he stepped further into the opening.

Max placed a finger under my chin and lifted my head, leaned in, and placed his mouth on mine. The kiss was soft and sweet, and left me wanting more when he pulled away.

"Be careful driving home," he said, then closed the door and tapped on the hood above before turning away to walk to his truck.

I latched my seatbelt and placed the vehicle in reverse and backed out. I looked in the rearview mirror as I moved the handle to drive and saw Max standing beside his truck watching me pull out.

"I definitely should have run," I said out loud as I pushed down on the gas petal. "Please don't let my heart hurt too long when he moves on," I added as I pulled out onto the main road.

Chapter Seven

Flirt

The backdoor opened just as I closed the kitchen drawer. I glanced over and grinned at my dad, Romeo, as he entered, and went back to unloading the dishwasher.

He set a container on the bar, then pulled a stool out and sat. I opened the cabinet where I kept my glasses and coffee cups and emptied the dishwasher's top shelf.

"What's in the container?" I asked while I finished unloading the few plates and putting them away.

"Leftovers from last night's dinner and dessert. Claire thinks you are going to starve," he said, and I chuckled.

"I'm all for her believing that. Keeps me from cooking. But I could do without the sweets. Unlike you, I can't afford the extra weight. I spend enough time at the gym to keep in shape for the women," I smirked, and my dad flipped me off.

"I haven't put on any weight, asshole," he sneered, which only made me smile wider.

"Keep telling yourself that, old man. When you need to replace the back shock on your bike, I don't want to hear you bitching."

"You're in an awfully good mood. Must have had a helluva night." My dad eyed me, and I stared back.

"It was alright," I said, not adding any extra about my night. I opened the refrigerator and pulled out a bottle of water. "You want something to drink?" I held the bottle of water up and asked.

"Nah, I'm good. I can't stay long. Claire's already left for the bakery, and I wanted to drop off the food before me and the others took off for a ride. The weather is clear today, and the temperature isn't bad. The storm we were supposed to get blew over, which was good. So we're going to take advantage and enjoy riding while we can." I knew he was talking about the dads when he said the others.

"Damn, if the guys and I weren't meeting up to discuss club business, I would tag along. It's been a while since I went out riding with no set place in mind," I said offhandedly as I uncapped the bottle of water and took a drink.

"Yeah, noticed you boys haven't been doing as much riding as you used to."

"Hard for Speed, Crusher, Devil, Ghost, and Jag to carve out time to ride between work, kids, and women." I finished the water and threw the empty bottle in the trash.

"You and Coast could have taken off. Nothing was tying the two of you down. Well, at least before Coast caught the doc, that is."

I shook my head. Since the dads had stepped down from the club's leadership, they had way too much time on their hands. I wasn't the least bit curious about how he knew Mac was at Coast's house.

"You and the other dads have turned into gossiping old women. Maybe we need to find you all something to do inside the club." I laughed at the look on my dad's face.

"Not a fucking chance in hell. We've done our time. If we want to sit on our asses or ride off when we have the notion, we've earned it. Besides, it's why we have you boys." He stood and pushed the stool back under the bar.

"Ah, finally the reason comes out of why we were kept," I said jokingly.

"Fuck no. We kept you pain in the asses because your mothers were batshit crazy. No sensible adult would have left one of you boys in their care," he said, shook his head, then stared me in the eyes. "I often wonder if your need to regulate everything in your life stems from the lack of control over your circumstances growing up. Each of you has handled your mothers' absences in different ways. But you've always been the more serious one. More often than not the one who had to be in control of what you and the others did or didn't do. What worries me is your relentless drive to circumvent letting others get too close to you."

"What are you talking about? I let others get close to me. Case in point my brothers." I waved my hand out and continued. "And that includes all my brothers, not just Speed, Crusher, Devil, Coast, and Jag. Ghost and I became good friends long before he joined the club," I said and frowned, not sure where my dad was going with his impromptu speech.

"Yet you have never let a single woman get close to you. I'm not talking about the closeness while you're fucking one or the friendship and brotherly feelings you have toward Sami, Carly, River, Bailey, Luna, and Mac."

"Oh, for fuck's sake. Don't tell me you think because I enjoy order in my life, a little kink with my sex or haven't had a serious relationship with a woman is from not having a mother present when I was growing up." I rubbed a hand down my face, then I started laughing. "How damn long have you been holding that one inside?"

"Don't be a dick. I'm your dad, and I have a right to worry when I see you pulling away from the others and spending a helluva lot of time by yourself. Especially when Coast went to Kiyaya's place. He's back now, but he's finally hooking up with Mac. Then I come in here, and you seem relaxed and happier than you have been in months, so I might have hoped…"

"It was because of a woman I met last night?" I finished for him and cocked a brow. "Christ, like I said before. You have all turned into little old women. So, if I tell you why I'm in a good mood, will you stop worrying?"

"As long as the answer isn't that you got laid. You've been having sex since you were fourteen and never looked more relaxed or happy than today. So…" My dad lift his hand palm up at me as if to say go ahead.

"First off, I don't want to know how you know I had sex at fourteen. Second, I seriously think you and the other dads need to find something to do to fill your free time because you really need more interests than what is happening in our lives," I said and held up my hand when my dad's eyes squinted and his mouth opened. "Third, if you and the other dads think the six of us suffered, acted out, or have underlying issues due to not having mothers around, you'd be wrong. My mother was a stripper with a drug problem, which if you hadn't stayed on top of while she was pregnant with me, I might not be here. I waste no energy thinking of what it would have been like to have her around while growing up.

"Was growing up in an MC traditional? No. Raised by just a dad or dads? Hell, a lot of kids are raised by single parents. Besides, we had Shakes. The woman couldn't have done a better job as a mother if she had birthed us herself. Each of you raised independent sons who got to grow up surrounded by many men that most young boys could only dream of having as role models. Not one of us suffered or wished our lives could have been different. Why the fuck would we? We had great childhoods.

"Now, granted, catching your dad doing a hang-around against the wall of the clubhouse probably wouldn't be considered the best example. However, it sure gave a twelve-year-old boy something to think about lying in bed at night," I said and laughed at the memory.

"Whatever, but you didn't get being an asshole from me. You must have picked that up from all the time you spent with Shakes," he said, and his lips twitched.

"Oh sure, we'll go with that if it makes you feel better. But to answer the main question, yes, I am in a good mood because of a woman. It's all you're getting."

"Fine, I can live with that. Though… I will add that if she turns out to be what you want—don't be a stubborn prick and fight it. You boys have heard us a thousand times say we never wanted to be strapped down with ol' ladies. But the more time I spend with Claire, I think we were young, wild, and a little stupid when we said it." He turned toward the door and reached for the doorknob, then glanced over his shoulder. "I shouldn't have to mention this, but I'm here if you need to talk."

"No, you don't. You have always been around to talk with," I answered, and when he opened the door and started to walk out, I added. "Thanks for the food. Next time you want to come over—don't feel as if you need an excuse to do so."

"I should have beaten your ass more," he mumbled.

I smiled and yelled, "Love ya, too, old man. Enjoy your ride and be safe," as the door shut behind him.

I was still grinning an hour later as I headed out the front door to go to the clubhouse and meet the others for Church.

Chapter Eight

Gabriella

"Mom, your cell phone is ringing!" I heard Sawyer yell as the washer buzzed, signaling the end of the cycle.

I walked out of the laundry room through the kitchen and into the living room where Sawyer laid on the floor, drawing and coloring while her favorite movie played on the TV.

"You could have brought it to me," I said as I reached for my cell that laid on the side table. I had left it there when I checked a load of laundry after the dryer timer buzzed.

Looking at the screen, I noticed the missed call was from my sister, Tori. With a couple of taps on the screen, the ringing started, and I waited for Tori to pick up.

"I'm not supposed to answer your phone," Sawyer answered without even looking up from her spot on the floor.

"Yeah, she's not supposed to answer your phone, Mom," Tori's voice funneled through the cell.

"Pfft. She may not answer it, but it never stops her from looking at the screen to see who's calling. So how's the public defender's life going? Did you get off any criminals this week?" I asked and pictured Tori rolling her eyes. She loved her job as an attorney for the Clark County Public Defender's office in Las Vegas, Nevada, to the dismay of our entire family.

"I know everyone thinks public defenders spend their days plotting how to get robbers, murderers, and rapists released. Unfortunately, it isn't that glamorous. An example would be yesterday. It consisted of three hookers picked up for solicitation and a homeless man picked up for shoplifting a couple of soap bars and a toothbrush and paste. If the excitement level stays steady, it could kill me," she said sarcastically, and I chuckled.

"Hey, if you were looking for everyday excitement, you could have gone to work for the family after law school," I teased.

"Ugh, as if dealing in business contracts and litigation daily would be stimulating. Not to mention working with family. Please, bring on the hardened criminals who can't afford an attorney," Tori griped, then in the next breath, changed the subject. "You're trying to sidetrack me, and it isn't going to work. You know why I am calling. Give it up, sister of mine. Did you or did you not go through with the rendezvous you had scheduled for last night?"

"Yes," I answered and stepped out of the living room. Sawyer might have looked engrossed in her activity and the television, but it didn't mean she wasn't listening.

"So how was it? And don't give me a one word answer. I want deets," she pushed.

"Why did I mention any of this to you?" I mumbled as I entered the laundry room.

"Because I'm your sister, and we have shared every milestone our whole lives. Besides, I have to live through you. It's been ages since I had a date. Even longer since I had sex. I'm to where even bad sex would work. Either that or I need to buy stock in every company that manufactures batteries."

"Good grief, Tori, I hear the violins playing. Why aren't you dating? You get asked out all the time," I reminded her.

"Oh yeah, by criminals."

"Stop it. You've told me other attorneys ask you out frequently," I stressed.

"Like I said. Criminals," she snidely answered, and I chuckled. "Laugh it up. They should consider some criminals for posing as decent human beings."

"Oh my God, are you still complaining about Edgar? You know not every man is like that. He was a lying, cheating creep, and it's been well over a year," I reasoned.

"Ugh, I am over it… mainly. I just can't bring myself to accept a date with another attorney. Christ, the man was dating me, two other women, and he was married, and the wife was pregnant. Who the fuck does that shit? Hell, maybe dating a criminal wouldn't be so bad. At least I'd know what I'd be dealing with."

"Well, between your job and family connections, you know quite a few of them," I joked.

"Girl, don't even go there. And stop changing the subject. Tell me about the guy." Tori was relentless. I supposed it was what made her an excellent attorney.

I placed the last folded towel in the laundry basket, then turned and leaned my butt against the dryer. "He's controlling, direct, sure of himself," I said and absently rubbed the palm of my hand across my breasts. There hadn't even been the slightest mark when I looked in the mirror this morning. It would have been relatively easy to convince myself nothing had taken place if not for the faint sign of whisker burn on the inside of one thigh, which I wouldn't have noticed if the hot water in my morning shower hadn't caused a tiny sting when it came in contact, making me take a closer look.

"Oh no, it was awful," Tori surmised when I hadn't continued.

"No. Yes. No. It was…" I paused, squeezed my eyes shut, and brought up Max's image, remembering how being with him felt. "It was the most intense sexual experience I have ever had, yet liberating at the same time. I'm not sure I can put into words how or what it felt like to have a man understand what I needed, not only physically but mentally. God, Tori, I loved Justin with my whole heart, and our sex life was incredible. After he was gone, the few times I have had sex, it was mediocre at best. It made me think it was me. Not that I expected it to be the same, especially with different partners. I had hoped for good. I could work with that, you know? When it wasn't, I chalked it up to maybe I wasn't ready to move on. I mean I was busy between finishing my internship and raising Sawyer, then moving here and starting my practice. After a bit, sex became… unimportant—something to concentrate on later when I had more free time.

"Then I finally feel ready to dip back into the relationship slash sexual pool because I was missing the intimacy two actual breathing individuals share, instead of having a battery-operated fill-in, and what happens? Every sleazy, overconfident, self-absorbed loser in a fifty-mile radius seems to be drawn to me. Which, hey, I might have been willing to overlook their less than stellar personalities for a crack-the-crystal-screaming-orgasm." I snorted, "But no. I get the bright idea I don't need the relationship part to reach sexual gratification, just a man. Because the characters in the books I started reading were having fulfilling and gratifying sexual encounters, so why couldn't that be me? I join a club because there isn't anything crazy about not knowing jack shit to do with BDSM other than from what I read in books. Oh, and the research on the internet where I decided I must be a submissive since letting a man push me sexually and take over allows me to reap the benefit without thinking sounded like something I would enjoy. For God's sake, I let a man I know absolutely nothing about... What was I thinking, Tori?"

"That you were lonely and carrying enough stress with your job and being a single parent, which doesn't leave enough time to have a personal life. Cut yourself a break. There's nothing wrong with you, Brie. Your reasons for joining a club might have been a little wacky, but you didn't just run out the door and find the first club to test your interest. You researched every aspect beforehand. You talked to me about it. Heck, you even texted the time you would be at the club, then texted when you were headed home just so someone would know where you were. I may not know much about sex clubs but, I know you. You are not the rash decision maker type. You never have been, which has me wondering. What is the cause behind your out-of-character little weirded-out moment?"

I sighed, opened my eyes, and pushed off the dryer. After positioning the phone between my ear and shoulder, I picked up the basket, planning to put away the laundry while I continued to talk with Tori.

"Brie, are you still there?" Tori asked as I walked out of the laundry room.

"Yeah, sorry. I don't know what came over me," I said, heading down the hallway toward the linen closet after a quick glance into the living room to make sure Sawyer was still occupied.

"I'll tell you what I think. I think something spooked you last night. Now, if you don't want my attorney mind running rapidly over every bad thing imaginable or my sister brain shouting go pack a bag and be ready to roll in case, my sister needs my help killing someone and hiding a body, then start explaining."

My sister could make me laugh no matter what was going on. "You sound like Gina. Maybe you really should have gone to work for the family."

"Yeah, yeah. Now get to talking."

"Nothing horrible took place, so you can relax," I said, then took a deep breath and blew it out before I continued. "I may have miscalculated on the mindless sexual escapade without a relationship."

"Oh."

"Yeah, oh. Tori, what started my tiny breakdown was… I might be a novice, but I'm not sure being an experienced submissive would have prepared me for Max," I said, lowering my voice as I passed the living room on my way back to the laundry room to return the empty basket to its place.

"Okay, it sounds like your first encounter went off with a bang or ended on a bang," Tori snickered, and I wanted to reach through the phone and smack her.

"Tori, it isn't funny."

"Fine. You used to be more fun before you unleashed your freaky side."

"I swear to God I will reach through this phone and snatch you bald if you don't stop it."

"Alright, alright, I'll stop. But I don't understand what the problem is. You evidently enjoyed yourself with this man. Enjoy yourself some more. Good sex could lead to a relationship. I don't know the club rules, but surely there isn't one that says you can't become involved outside the club. Is there?"

"No. It's just this was supposed to be physical without all the other stress from being in a relationship. Crud, I am overthinking this. It was one time. Who's saying the next time won't be a dud? He could have been on his 'A' game since it was our first experience together." Even as I spoke, I didn't believe a word of it.

"Uh huh, keep saying it, and you might even believe it. So you are meeting up with him again, I presume, since you said next time. Can I give you a bit of advice? If you decide you want more than earth shattering orgasms, then go after it. I can't think of anyone who deserves to have everything more than you, my sister."

"You are going to make me cry. God, I miss you, Tori. I can't wait to see and spend time with you during the holidays," I said and wiped the corner of my eye with a finger to keep the lone tear from sliding out.

"I get the whole moving there and stuff, but I sure miss having you close. Especially since you insisted on taking Sawyer with you. Now let me talk with my favorite niece before we hang up."

"Love ya, sis. Talk to you later," I said before reaching the living room and handing the phone off to Sawyer.

While Tori and Sawyer talked, I took care of another laundry load and made a pass through the house, picking up the mess from the previous week. I was headed back into the living room when I ran into Sawyer in the doorway. My cell rang as she held it out to me. I looked at the screen and groaned. It was my service calling, which was never a good sign on the weekend.

Chapter Nine

Flirt

As I walked out of the house, the others were doing the same, and we converged in the middle of the road.

"Think we should knock on Coast's door?" Jag asked.

"Nah, I'm sure he'll show up," I said and started walking. No way I was going to be the one to interrupt him, considering how long it had taken him to get Mac inside his house.

"I hope he doesn't think he got Mac to his house with no one noticing," Speed said and shook his head. "Ally hears pipes, and she is in her window. Took her less than five seconds to run downstairs to tell Sami that she spotted Mac was on the back of Coast's bike."

"Because she is nosey like her aunt. Carly does the same shit, and since the house sits at the end, I'm surprised her nose print isn't on all the front windows," Crusher said and laughed.

"What's wrong with you, Dev?" I asked when I noticed he hadn't said anything, and for Devil that was very unusual.

"Brother, you still can't be mad," Speed mentioned, and Devil sneered at him.

My lips twitched, but I held off my laughter and asked, "What has you mad, man?"

"I missed the UFC match last night,' he grouched.

"Oh yeah, I heard on the radio coming home it was an outstanding showdown. Both fighters were equally matched, and it went down to the wire," I commented as we reached the clubhouse and waited for Crusher to unlock the backdoor. "How did you miss it? Every day for the last month that's all they talked about on the radio and television."

Jag snorted and earned himself a sneer from our brother. Whatever had Devil upset had to be good.

"Since Neely got in trouble at school for punching that little jerkoff, Bailey wouldn't let me turn the fight on last night. Not sure how my sister getting in trouble turns into me getting punished in my house, but go figure. I was planning to go to one of their freaking houses to watch it. However, the warden had already told the other women," Devil explained, and I wasn't able to hold in the laughter any longer.

We were still laughing when we stopped inside the clubhouse for Crusher to unlock the doors to the large room that had been renovated specifically to handle a full member Church. Today would only be the six of us.

"I wasn't home, but why didn't you use your key and go to my house and watch the fight?" I brought up as we walked into the room once the double doors were opened.

"Sonofabitch!" Devil said as he walked past me, pulled out a seat at the table, and plopped down on it. Then he dropped his forehead onto the surface. "How could I forget that?"

I pulled out a chair along with the others, and we joined Devil at the table. "Brother, do you really want one of us to answer that?" I asked, and the others chuckled when Devil flipped a middle finger without raising his head.

After a few more minutes of giving Devil a hard time, the door opened, and Coast walked in.

"Well, look who decided to join us. Takes a week off, then saunters in all loose hipped," Jag teased, and the rest of us laughed.

"Yeah, you'd think he'd be wearing a smile instead of a scowl," Devil added.

"Who wants to make a bet? I say he not only makes Mac an ol' lady. I got a hundred says he'll take it all the way and be married by Christmas," I said and chuckled when Coast flipped me off. Which only moved the earlier ribbing of Devil in his direction.

"I'll take that bet. But I say he won't wait around like some have, and he'll have a ball and chain before Christmas," Jag said.

"Hey, Sami is the one who won't set up a time. I put a ring on her finger. That counts," Speed said and glared at Jag.

"Carly's got my ring on her finger, too. She's my ol' lady, and that has just as much if not more meaning than a piece of paper," Crusher argued.

I leaned back in my chair and smiled, ready to enjoy the show because with my brothers, they were relentless as dogs with a bone.

"Bailey wants to wait until the baby is born," Devil said.

"Fuck all of you. I'm going to take it slow with Mac. I don't want to push too hard and have to chase her down again," Coast said, which only set off another round of laughter.

"Yeah, I definitely want in on the bet. Coast being patient—that would be a first," Devil added, and I made a fist and stretched my arm across the table. Devil did the same, and we bumped fists.

"Put me down for a hundred for before Halloween," Jag said.

"Me, too. Make mine before Thanksgiving. I'll give him a little time," Crusher said.

"Oh, shit. You have to get married on Thanksgiving," Devil said and laughed.

I lifted a brow and looked at him, then at Coast, who was frowning. At least I wasn't the only one who didn't understand.

"What the hell does Thanksgiving have to do with Mac and I marrying?" Coast inquired, and I almost groaned seeing the look Devil gave him. The look screamed something inappropriate was likely going to come out of his mouth.

"Oh, come on, work with me. It would be cool as hell to have you get married before the club's big Thanksgiving dinner. You already have the part of the Indian covered, and Mac only needs to find a Pilgrim dress."

I ran my hand down my face and shook my head. Though I held off on groaning, the others didn't.

"Something is seriously wrong with you, Dev," Speed said.

"You're such a dumbass," Coast said as he sat down beside Devil and shoved him.

Devil righted himself in the chair. "You know it was a joke, right? I love you, brother."

"Of course I know it was a joke. You still have your hair, don't you?" Coast asked and chuckled while the others and I laughed.

"Hey! Why are you laughing at his scalping remark, and you didn't laugh at mine?" Devil asked, acting disgruntled as he looked around the table at the rest of us.

"Because we weren't laughing at the comment. We were picturing you without hair," I answered since I was the first to get myself under control.

"No one touches the hair. Well, except Bailey when she grabs hold of it while I'm eat—"

"Stop!" Speed yelled and cut our brother off. "Have you been hanging around Roscoe?"

"No more than usual. Why?" Devil asked.

"Never mind. I'll repeat, you have issues, brother," Speed said and shook his head.

Devil shrugged and replied, "Like you just figured that shit out." Which had us all laughing again. At this rate, we weren't going to get anything done.

Finally, Crusher called the meeting to order, and we started going over business. The only business I didn't have information on was the construction business Ghost and Dare ran. Ghost would stop by and give an update on how it was doing. This meeting was for us, the leadership, to put together everything discussed when we held the next full member Church.

The club had grown since we took over, which wasn't a reflection on our dads' reign. We had added more businesses and brought in more prospects to help with the minor jobs no one had the time to deal with.

"Whenever you're ready, Flirt," Crusher said.

"Well, overall, the club is doing excellent. We are going to exceed the profit margin goal we set for the bike shop. Roscoe has the pawnshop running smooth, and it should hit an all-time high this year. Hell, we are sustaining our income even with Soft Tails' stripping side closed right now. The bar side business has picked up since we separated it from the strip side. The people in town love the food, and the place is staying busy. When the strip side opens back up, profits should skyrocket, covering the cost of the renovations. If my calculations are right, the club should have a ten percent profit increase across the board," I finished.

"Tank's doing great managing Soft Tails. Between Luna helping him line up new talent and Sami teaching him the books. Depending on how the showcase strippers go, we might have to hire an assistant for him. He can't spend all his time in the office," Jag said.

I nodded in agreement. Tank was too valuable to be hidden away in an office under mounds of paperwork.

Crusher took over next and brought new business to the table concerning Yoga Sensual, the business in the same building as the club run gym. Willa, the lady who owned the business, was struggling to make ends meet and was going to look for another place cheaper to rent. While he continued to talk, I started running through different avenues the club could go if we lost Yoga Sensual as a tenant. It wasn't just about the rent we took in. The women took yoga classes from Willa and bought sensual oils and other products from her, too. When I finally focused back on the surrounding conversation, I shook my head and grinned. It seemed the brothers had gone off track once again. As I listened and even added my own opinions, for a second, I wondered if there was any truth to my dad's worry about the effects not having mothers around had on the six of us. Because as I laughed at some of the shit being said, none of us had the right to give Devil a hard time about having issues. Hell, maybe we did, too.

Forcing myself to focus back on club business, I raised my hand, looked at Crusher, and said, "Hold up. How does Stroker know all that about Willa's business?"

The brother sighed. "He's seeing her. I didn't want to bring that up yet and have it become a factor in anyone's decision on what we should do."

As the club's VP, Jag spoke while the rest of us digested what Crusher revealed. "I am going to play devil's advocate and ask. Is he seriously seeing her, or is she just the person he's fucking right now?"

I watched Crusher run his hand down his face and knew I needed to work something out that not only would help Willa but the club, too. When he answered, I knew I had read him right.

"Seriously seeing her. That is not me just saying it because he is my dad. He has never hidden any… conquest… for lack of a better word. However, I'm not sure he wouldn't still be hiding the relationship if I hadn't gone to the place to pay for Carly's classes and caught him and Willa together."

"Damn, another one of them down. I find it humorous every time I see my dad with Claire. But it is nice to see him relaxed and happy," I said.

"I couldn't agree more. It's just a bonus to give them shit about it. But back to not thinking of your dad and Willa's relationship as being a factor. It is," Coast brought up but quickly added. "Club takes care of its own. We always have." He was right. If Stroker was serious about Willa, then the club would do everything we could.

"Have Stroker tell Willa to hold off a bit. Let me run some numbers. We might be able to do away with charging her rent if we offer her clientele packages from our massage side. We could make the most of what we lose on her rent from that side. The club wouldn't be out of anything except potential profits. Leaving us where we are right now." I shrugged.

"Alright, run the numbers, Flirt. I'll let my dad know to talk to Willa. Anyone have an issue with looking into helping her?" Crusher asked.

"No, like Coast said before. We take care of our own. If the numbers don't work out that way, then we find another way," Jag said, and the rest of us agreed.

"Okay then, now let's finish this up. Ghost should be here in five," Crusher said, and we finished going over the last of the business when someone knocked on the door. Coast got up and went to the door. When he opened it, Ghost stood on the other side.

Coast asked Ghost how he was doing, and I grinned when he answered, "Great." Then asked Coast, "They tell you I'm going to have two boys?"

The brother had been walking on air since he found out. Ghost was another one who was more relaxed and happier. Which I was glad to see. Luna coming back into his life had changed everything for the better.

As they walked across the room toward us, Coast asked Ghost about windows and roofing material for his great grandfather's place. Even though the place was small, Coast was going to need more than just his dad's help.

"I can help," I offered.

"I don't need to tell you the rest of us will help if you need us," Crusher volunteered.

"Appreciate it. But with my dad and Flirt, we should be good," Coast said.

"Just let us know," Jag added.

Ghost talked, and we all listened as he filled us in on the gym, and the massage place's progress, which both would be ready to be opened by the end of next month. The BHMC Dispensary would be ready in two weeks. The club

90

was only waiting on the final approval and license from the state.

We all walked out together after the meeting ended. Ghost pointed at his truck. "You guys want to pile in? I figured since I didn't see any bikes around you must have walked."

"Nah, brother. Go home to your woman; we're good," I answered for all of us.

"I'm going that way, anyway. I need to pick Luna up. I dropped her at your house, Speed, but I'm sure she's probably at yours with the others," Ghost said and pointed at Coast.

"The others? Hell, how do they know Mac is at my house? When we rode in last night, it was dark, and no one was out. The only person who saw us was Flirt," Coast said and looked around, then focused on me.

"Wasn't me," I said and held my hands up in surrender. I tried not to laugh at the look of distress on Coast's face. The brother had every right to be worried about the women converging on his house. It was precisely one of the many reasons I enjoyed keeping my personal business close to my chest. It wasn't just the interrogations the brothers would put me through. The women would be three times worse and not nearly as stealth in trying to gather information.

When Ghost laughed, I looked toward him. "I'm glad I live on the other side, but if the club ever falls short on cash, we could start a reality show like the *Hollywood Wives* and call it—The Women of Black Hawk."

I chuckled. The brother hit that nail on the head. "They don't miss much, that's for sure. And, brother, I'm not even going to ask how you know anything about a show called *Hollywood Wives.*"

"My bet would be Bailey. The yesterday you left right after she mentioned Mac was at the hospital because of an emergency." Devil shrugged when Coast glared at him.

"All I know is when I was outside cleaning the back of my truck out, Luna opened the door with her cell to her ear and asked if I would drop her off at Sami's on my way here. So that's what I did. When I pulled up in front of Speed's house, Carly was walking in the front door. And no, I didn't ask Luna why she wanted to be dropped off. I've learned I'm better off not knowing," Ghost said, then glanced at each of us. "A lift or not?"

In the end, the seven of us squeezed into Ghost's crew cab. Just because I kept my business to myself didn't mean I didn't enjoy watching one of my brothers get roasted by the women. Besides, he could end up needing help to track Mac down if the women scared her off.

Chapter Ten

Flirt

We reached Coast's house, and I stayed by the front door when we entered. With everything that was said after we walked in, it seemed Coast should have been more worried about the women rubbing off on Mac.

"I found out today that evidently there are some things that stay private around here," Mac said and jumped when I threw back my head and laughed.

From Mac's statement, it seemed as if I had even made it into their conversation. I sobered up and looked at Mac. "That there is, Mac," I said, then turned my attention to Coast. "Happy for you, brother." I honestly was happy for him. He had been after Mackenzie for a while, and if dealing with the women hadn't sent her running today, all would be good.

The women and men, with the kids leading the way, started walking toward the door, and I reached back for the handle and opened the door so they could walk out. When I looked down, a set of dark brown eyes stared up at me. They were set in the face of a little girl I had never seen before, but looked vaguely familiar at the same time.

"Who do you belong to?" she asked me, and my brows creased as I studied her features.

"Who do you belong to?" I casually asked.

Instead of answering me, she said, "I asked first."

"Come on, Sawyer. Let's get back to the house," Sami said and moved closer to the door, then placed one hand on Ally's shoulder and the other on the little girl's, she had called Sawyer.

"He don't belong to anyone. That's my uncle Flirt," Ally told her friend.

Sawyer's eyebrows drew together, never taking her eyes off me and asked, "What's wrong with you? Are you one of those men who is interested in younger women? Or don't you have a job?"

My lips twitched as my brothers chuckled. It hit me that Sawyer was the kid who got into trouble with Ally and Neely at school. The one they had also said asked a shit ton of questions.

"Ah, you're the interrogator," I said. It was what Devil had labeled her.

"What's that?" she asked.

"Yeah, she the ped's daughter," Devil interjected.

"The one in the building next to Mac's?" I asked.

"Yes, her pediatric practice is next to mine," Mac answered.

As I continued to look at Sawyer, I realized who she looked like. Damn it, I was glad I came to Coast's house. "To answer your questions, Sawyer. I don't belong to anyone. But I am hoping I'll get to change that soon. And there's nothing wrong with me. I even have a job."

She nodded her head. "That's good. Women like those things. You're pretty, too. Everybody needs someone. My mom does. She don't have a husband."

Sawyer seemed to be a lot like Ally, no filter. I wished her mother had the same problem. Gabriella shared the bare minimum. The only thing I learned about her—other than sexually—was she had a child.

"Well, now I know why Sawyer and Ally hit it off. Let's go," Speed said, chuckling as he reached for the door, pulling it open further.

I smiled at Sawyer, and the skin at the corner of her eyes crinkled when she smiled back at me. I had a feeling if I ever saw a picture of Gabriella at Sawyer's age, I wouldn't be able to see a difference.

Everyone filed out of Coast's house, and since I was last, I pulled the door shut behind me.

"Can you show us some fighting moves now, Dev?" Neely asked as soon as everyone was on the road in front of Coast's house.

"Sure," Devil answered and did the brother and sister weird face palm when he bent and picked Neely up.

Bailey sighed. "Really, Lance? You can't be serious about teaching her to fight. I hope you enjoyed going to meet with the principal because you and she are going to become friends by the time Neely gets through elementary school."

"I'm going to show her defensive moves so she can protect herself. She doesn't need to learn how to throw a punch. My sister has that down pat," Devil bragged, and then he and Neely awarded Bailey with twin smiles.

"I get to learn, too, Uncle Devil. Right, Daddy?" Ally asked, looking up at Speed with hopeful eyes I knew would make it impossible for him to say no.

"They should know how to protect themselves," Speed said as he looked at Sami.

She stuck her hand up. "I will not bother arguing. Just know next time you will sit beside Devil in the principal's office," she said.

"I'm going home to take a nap," Bailey said and turned toward her and Devil's house.

"Well, since my girl isn't old enough, which I am eternally grateful for right now, I'm going home," Jag said and slung his free arm over River's shoulder as they walked toward their place with Poppy bouncing on his hip, waving her hand at us.

"Carly has to get ready for her shift," Crusher said and started leading Carly away.

"Are you trying to get rid of me? I have like two hours before I need be in," we heard Carly say, then heard her squeal when Crusher smacked her on the ass. It wasn't hard to guess what Crusher had in mind for the extra time before Carly reported to the station.

"Going home and laying down sounds like a brilliant plan," Luna mentioned. Then she and Ghost said goodbye and loaded Karma into his truck and left.

With the brothers having things to do with their families, I would either go home, go to town, or go to the bike shop and work on the bikes we had started building. I would have rather been riding, though, and wished I hadn't had the earlier meeting, I could have gone out with the dads.

"Are you going to help, Uncle Flirt?" Ally asked, and as I prepared to tell her I had plans, she added. "You could help Sawyer so it would be even."

I glanced at Sawyer, who stood beside Sami with her eyes glued to me. Hopefulness reflected from their chocolate depths, leaving me with no choice. I swear all females were born with the knowledge of what that look could get them from a man. I had a feeling between her and Gabriella, they would reel me in with little effort. It wouldn't take either of them long. If Sawyer were my daughter, I would be in worse shape than Speed.

"Yeah, I got time to show you girls a few things. It would be irresponsible as a former Navy SEAL to leave your training up to the Army," I found myself saying and grinned when Speed and Devil glared at me. They would have had more to say for sure if the girls hadn't been there.

"Well, let's get to it," Speed said, and the little girls cheered. We all started walking toward Speed's house.

"I think I'm going to take Bailey's lead and lay down while you guys entertain the girls. Which will happen in the backyard and not inside the house," Sami instructed. "And if one of them gets hurt, I will not be happy. Nor will Bailey and Brie," she warned as she stepped up onto the porch.

"Did you forget I was a medic in the Army?" Devil questioned.

"Not at all," Sami replied over her shoulder, then opened the door, walked in, and shut it behind her.

"Is it me, or are the pregnancies making the women meaner?" Devil asked in a voice barely above of a whisper as if he were afraid Sami would hear and come back out of the house.

Speed and I answered at the same time, "You." Then we started laughing.

Instead of cutting through the house, we started around the side of it toward the back. Devil put Neely back on her feet, and the three girls took off running ahead of us.

"How did you guys get roped into this?" I asked and saw Speed give Devil a scathing look.

"Hey, what was I supposed to do?" Devil asked Speed, who shook his head.

"Not promise them we would teach them. You know Ally forgets nothing, so of course, she has asked me every single day," Speed said disgustedly.

"They caught me off guard, and it was the only thing I could come up with. Would you rather I signed them up for classes instead?" Devil barked back at Speed.

"What classes?" I asked, my curiosity peaked by the brothers' tones and facial expressions.

"Devil stopped by the gym the other day and he had Ally and Neely with him. Ghost and a few of the other brothers were practicing Krav Maga. The girls asked if they could take classes. Instead of telling them they were too young, he told Neely and Ally they needed to check with me, Bailey, and Sami. But in the meantime, he and I could show them a thing or two," Speed grouched as we reached the backyard.

I snorted, "Brothers, you are so whipped."

"F you. I am not the only one who can't tell them no," Devil sneered.

"Might be true, but you're the one using letters instead of dropping the 'F' bomb. Face it, short people who wear dresses control the club," I said and glanced toward the girls and grinned. The three were in a circle and bent at the waist with their fingertips touching the ground.

"You ladies stretching?" I asked as my lips twitched.

"Yep. Uncle Ghost said you could pull a muscle if you don't," Ally said, then the three raised up and made the same move again.

"It probably won't work. We don't got muscles," Sawyer said as she stood, then bent her arm and poked a finger on her nonexistent biceps.

"We can get muscles. You got to lift weights," Neely brought up while placing one leg out in front of her body and bending at the knee and leaning toward it. I lifted a brow at Devil.

"What? She stretches with me before I run," Devil said and shrugged.

"When did you start running?" I asked and noticed Speed and Devil exchange looks.

"Uh, like two or three months ago. I've been running with Ghost a couple times a week," Devil answered.

"Oh," was the only response there was to give.

"You would have known if you were around more," Speed said as he stepped off the back porch with a rolled-up mat.

"Is that from the gym?" I asked as I grabbed an end and helped him carry it out into the grass.

"Yeah, I swung by there last night and grabbed it. We have a few extras in the back," Speed answered as we unrolled it on the lawn. When we stood, Speed waved Ally over.

"What did you mean if I was around more? I'm always around." I got a bad feeling. The thought that my dad might have been right when he mentioned me pulling away struck hard.

Devil verified it when he answered, "Don't get your panties in a wad. We get you and Coast are unattached and don't want to spend your free time with the rest of us. Well, at least you both used to be single. By the looks of things today, you are the only one left. Anyhow, we get it."

"You are spouting bullshit," I said and pulled my wallet out from my back pocket, opened it, and handed Ally a dollar.

"You wouldn't be getting pissed if you really thought it was bull," Speed said with a smug look on his face, which I would have liked to knock off if not for three little girls watching and listening to us.

"We should get started." I waved my hand out to the six of us standing around the mat. "Before I have to pay Ally more money."

"I'm going to make lots of money being a fighter," Neely said.

"How are you going to be a fighter? They don't wear girly clothes," Ally responded, and Neely frowned at her.

"They do when they're not fighting," Neely said, then looked at Devil. "Right, Dev?"

I concentrated on the girls and found it easy to let go of being mad. More than likely, because the brothers had been spot-on with their assessment, and I hadn't wanted to analyze it. Even more so, I had no plans to acknowledge any of it to them.

"Sure do, sis," Devil agreed with Neely, and she smiled.

"Well, I don't like dresses," Ally said.

"I do," Neely said pointedly.

"Do you like them, Sawyer?" Ally asked.

"Nothin' wrong with them. 'Cept when you wear 'em grownups always say to act like a lady," Sawyer said, and her upper lip curled in disgust.

My lips twitched as I listened to the debate on dresses. It was like watching small women with different tastes in clothing. Neely wore a multicolored skirt with leggings under it and a light pink sweatshirt that matched. While Ally looked as if she stepped out of a biker clothing catalog for kids. Sawyer had on jeans and a purple sweatshirt.

Ally looked up at Speed. "I'm gonna be a mechanic, so I can fix my bike by myself. Mechanics don't wear girly stuff," she declared.

"Yeah, yeah, I'm sure your momma will be pleased to hear that," Speed replied sarcastically.

"No happier than Bailey was when she heard Neely wanted to be in the MMA," Devil said.

I looked between the two of them and shook my head. "See. Whipped," was all I said and laughed when they flipped me off from behind the girls so they wouldn't see them.

"Alright, let's get started," Speed said, then moved to Ally. Devil moved to Neely, and I moved to stand in front of Sawyer.

"What do you want to be when you grow up, Sawyer? A doctor like your mom?" I asked her. Before she answered, Speed told the girls to turn around.

"Okay, you are going to pretend we are strangers and show us what you would do if we walked up behind you and grabbed you," Speed explained and moved closer to Ally and placed a hand on her shoulder. Devil did the same with Neely.

When I moved closer to Sawyer and placed my hand on her shoulder, she chose that second to answer me.

"A cop," she said matter-of-factly.

I grinned. The two seemed to share more than looks. Sawyer possessed the same quality her mother had when asked a question. Short and to the point answers. No explanation and nothing extra.

I opened my mouth to ask her why she wanted to be a cop, but the words never had time to cross my lips. Sawyer stomped on my foot and swung her arm back, her pointy little elbow making a direct hit to my groin. My brain registered the pain, and I dropped to my knees, one hand on the ground to hold me up while the other went to the crotch of my pants. Stars flickered behind my eyes, and I groaned.

"Girls, that's how you take down a Navy SEAL," Devil said, his voice laced with humor.

I squeezed my eyes shut, gritted my teeth, and promised myself I would kill him as soon as the nausea subsided.

Chapter Eleven

Gabriella

"I'm sorry we ruined your day, Dr. Agassi. You didn't need to come in and check on her. We should have brought her straight to the ER instead of calling your service. But when I couldn't get the gummy out of Dana's nose, and she started crying, struggling to breathe, I panicked. If I had taken a few seconds to think, I would have remembered it was the weekend," Beth Michaels apologized for what felt like the hundredth time since I walked into the exam room.

"Again, it wasn't a problem. I knew she would be taken care of in the ER. I just wanted to come check on Dana to make sure the asthma attack was indeed because of being upset over the stuffed-up nose. Not her medication dosage being too low."

"Dana hasn't had an attack since you prescribed meds for her. She didn't get upset today until we tried to get the gummies out ourselves," Mr. Michaels said from beside his wife. "Who knew a three-year-old's nostril was that deep?"

I smiled at Mr. Michaels. "Oh, you would be surprised what they can fit up the nose and in their ears. It all ended well, and she's going to be fine. That is the important thing."

"Thank God. Took ten years off my life," Beth said while she looked down at Dana, who was asleep on the bed.

"I'm going to head out. A nurse will come back with Dana's discharge paperwork once Dr. Booker signs off on it. Have a good weekend and watch those gummies." The Michaels' smiled, and after they said goodbye, I walked out of the room.

As I walked toward the exit doors, I pulled my phone out and checked for any missed messages or calls. I slipped it into my back jean pocket and reached in my front pocket for my keys.

"Heading home, Brie?"

If I hadn't been standing in the middle of the ER, I would have groaned out loud. Yet, I wasn't able to stop rolling my eyes before I turned my head toward the nurses' station and the person who spoke.

"Dr. Booker," I acknowledged with a forced smile.

"Did you find anything wrong with my medical assessment? We could go to the cafeteria for coffee and discuss it."

Good grief, what had I seen in the man to accept a dinner invitation? Loneliness was the reason. New town, no friends, just acquaintances, so I accepted his offer for dinner and regretted it five minutes after we had sat down at the table that evening. I hadn't answered any of his calls, and I avoided him when I came to the hospital as much as professionally possible. It was my bad luck he was working the ER today.

I ignored the first part of his statement and addressed the second. "Sorry, no time for coffee. I'm a little rushed for time," I easily lied and without waiting for a response, I turned and continued to the exit doors. It seemed easier than politely standing there when I knew it would be only a matter of time before he brought up the unanswered calls. Or the messages he'd left for more dinner invites. I had hoped my lack of interest would have him moving on to the next woman.

I reached my car, opened the door and got in. By the time I pulled out of the parking lot, I had placed the last couple of hours out of my mind and focused on the road. Last night's activity, coupled with the regular weekend morning and chores, had tiredness creeping in.

Once I picked Sawyer up at Sami's house, maybe we would grab some takeout and then veg on the couch and watch a movie or two for the rest of the day.

"Do you know Ally's dad and Neely's da… brother was in the Army?" Sawyer asked, then sucked the Lo Mein noodle into her mouth before it slipped from the chopsticks she was determined to eat with.

"As a matter of fact, I do," I answered and shook my head when Sawyer stabbed a chopstick into a piece of chicken. "You sure you wouldn't rather use a fork?"

"Nope," she said and bit the chicken off the end and chewed. "Flirt is a SEAL." She added, stabbing another piece of meat.

"You mean he *was* a SEAL, sweetie? The men are no longer in the military."

"I know, but Flirt said once a SEAL, always a SEAL. He said Speed and Devil were eni… envious."

"He did, huh? What did Speed and Devil say to that?" I asked as I closed the container of rice. When Eleanor hadn't been home for me to ask if she could watch Sawyer while I ran to the hospital, I planned to take Sawyer with me and let her sit in a chair at the nurses' station while I checked on Dana. Instead, it worked out for the better when, as we were getting ready to leave the house, Sami called and invited Sawyer to come play with Ally.

Flirt was the only one I hadn't met out of the group, but evidently, he had made a big impression on my daughter because she had talked about him the entire car ride back to town after I had picked her up at Sami's house. She continued talking about him while we were in the Chinese place waiting for our food order. When we came into the house, she'd finally run out of things to say about him. At least it was what I thought.

"Yep. They called him a dick, and then they both handed Ally a dollar. Is dick a bad word? Ain't it a man's name?" Sawyer asked.

I slapped my chest and coughed, then reached for my glass and took a large drink.

"Well, it can be a name and also a bad word," I answered, didn't bother to correct her on using the word *ain't*, and hoped she'd accept the response and drop it—no such luck.

"Then what's it mean?"

"Sometimes men or boys will use it to refer to their private parts," I explained the easiest way I knew how.

"Oh."

"Yes, oh. But it isn't something little girls should say or repeat," I stressed.

"Okay."

"Are you finished, sweetie?" I asked, changing the subject, and reached for one of the other open containers on the table.

"Uh huh. Are we going to watch a movie now?"

"As soon as I put the food away," I said and moved around the kitchen, doing just that.

I woke with credits from the movie running and looked to the other end of the couch to a sleeping Sawyer. After I turned the television off, I moved to pick Sawyer up. She hadn't moved once until I laid her down on her bed.

"Is the movie over?" she asked as I pulled the blankets up.

"Yeah, we both fell asleep before it was over. Night, sweetie. See you in the morning." I kissed her forehead, then started to leave her room.

"Flirt has a job and is really nice. He doesn't have a wife or any kids," Sawyer said, which stopped me in my tracks.

"Honey, not every person gets married or has kids. And that is great he has a job." I stood at the door and wondered where she was going with her newest infatuation.

"But I think he wants some," she mumbled sleepily and turned on her side. I didn't move, nor did I respond. Honestly, I didn't know what to say, so I stood there to make sure she was asleep. I grabbed the knob on her door, but before I pulled it closed behind me, she spoke again. "He looked kind of sad when Speed kissed Sami while she was fixing lunch. And he held Poppy when Jag came outside after her nap. Plus, he helped me learn fighting stuff."

"Fighting stuff?" I inquired and wondered if Sawyer was recalling some weird dream she had while asleep on the couch.

"Uh huh. He worked with me while Speed helped Ally and Devil helped Neely. He even wasn't mad when I hit him with my elbow."

"You hit him with your elbow?"

"Yep, right between the legs. After he stood back up, he told me I'd done a good job. Even Devil said that was how you took down a Navy SEAL. Flirt didn't get mad at me, but he gave Devil a mean face." In the dim light, I saw Sawyer yawn and close her eyes.

"Go to sleep, sweetie. You can tell me more tomorrow."

"'K." I stepped out of the room and started pulling the door closed. "Mom?"

"Yeah, sweetie."

"Do you think you might get married one day, and I can have another daddy since I never got to meet mine?"

"Maybe one day, Sawyer. It sure will have to be someone special if I'm going to have to share you," I forced out through the lump that had formed in my throat.

"'K. Love you, Mom."

"Love you, too, sweetie," I said and closed the door to her room.

Once I reached my room, I closed the door and slipped into my bed, and shed a few tears. It didn't matter that Sawyer rarely mentioned anything about not having a dad around, but when she did, it tore me to pieces knowing how much she and I both had lost. She would have been Justin's world.

Was there another man out there who would not only fall in love with me but Sawyer, too? With that thought, I closed my eyes and readied myself to relive moments of Justin in my dreams like any other time he was fresh in my mind when I went to bed. Instead, Max's face appeared, and as sleep pulled me under, my dreams were filled with what could be and not what had been.

Chapter Twelve

Flirt

Several months later...

"Are you testing the durability of that wrench or the concrete floor, Flirt?"

"What?" I looked over my shoulder at Coast and asked.

"Something bothering you?" Devil questioned, then pointed at the wrench beside me. "That tool, along with every other one you have used today, has been slammed or tossed around. Not to mention you've been mumbling shit as you abuse the tools."

"What are you talking about? I haven't been mumbling or abusing tools," I grouched.

"Acting like a man with woman troubles," Jag said from his spot across the garage.

I snatched up the rag and pushed myself off the floor. "Woman troubles? I've never had woman troubles. You must have me confused with yourself," I sneered as I wiped my hands with the rag.

"Going straight to the defensive. What's up with that?" Crusher pointed out and chuckled when I narrowed my eyes at him.

"Definitely a woman," Speed snorted. "Only reason a man gets that prickly with his friends."

"Prickly. Christ, every one of you has gone soft!" I shouted. I knew I was being an ass and couldn't bring myself to care. "Do your ol' ladies lock your balls up at night and then give them back to you in the morning?" I threw out and started toward the door. "I am allowed to have a bad day, so fuck off, assholes."

"See, now that's the thing, Flirt. All the time I have known you, I have never seen you lose control. And, brother, we have been in some shitty situations where losing control would have made the mission a lot easier for us," Ghost said as he walked into the garage.

"None of you know what you're talking about. We don't spend, nor have we spent, 24/7 together. Like everyone else, I have bad days. I am out of here. I'll be back when you all decide to work and not dick around." I walked out of the garage and stormed up Speed's driveway. When I reached my house, I stomped up the steps onto the porch. I opened the front door, then slammed it shut. In the living room, I plopped down on the couch and leaned my head back.

"I am still in control. They don't know what the hell they're talking about," I said out loud into the empty room, then closed my eyes. Even the breathing exercises I used when I felt any semblance of my control slipping were not helpful. Oh, they cleared my mind, but the control I fought to gain back was out of reach. The fault belonged to one woman. She had my gut twisted, but I refused to bring it up

110

or even acknowledge to my brothers they were right about a woman causing my foul mood.

"Definitely not ready to listen to them throw every word I have ever said about what would happen when I found the woman perfect for me. And certainly not that I've had her in my reach for months and done nothing to lock her down."

"Damn, months, huh?"

I ran a hand down my face, then opened my eyes and raised my head off the couch. "For fuck's sake, did those bastards call and tattle to my *daddy*?" I sneered.

"Goddamn, you *are* in a foul mood," my dad said as he walked through the room and then into the kitchen. I heard the refrigerator door open and the rattle of glass before it closed, and then he walked back into the living room. He handed me a beer, then went to the chair and sat down. "Now, you want to tell your *daddy* about this perfect woman you've known for months?"

I flipped my dad off, and he chuckled. Then I twisted the cap on my bottle of beer and took a long pull. "I'm not sure one beer is going to do," I admitted.

"If we run out, I have some over at my house."

"Good, if I don't need it during explaining, I might need it after. I've fucked up, Dad. Big time," I said, then started telling my dad about the first time I met Gabriella.

"Christ, son, when you mess up, you do it on a big scale that's for sure," my dad said, set the bottle of beer in his hand on the table beside the chair, and shook his head.

I sat forward and rested my bent arms across the top of my legs while my hands hung between. "Yeah, I know. I also know some of the frustration I am feeling stems a little from a deep-seated worry that when she finds out, she'll walk."

"You know you should have spoken to her at the beginning, so I can save my breath there. I agree with your assessment of fucking up big time, and I don't think anyone has to tell you to come clean immediately. Don't wait until you meet up again. Then you're going to have to stand and take your hits like every other man who's done crazy shit when it's come to a woman. My advice is to get everything out in the open. Let her take her pound of flesh, then after she calms down, lock her ass down."

I stared at my dad and cocked a brow. "That's your advice."

"Yes, it is," he answered and stared back at me.

"I agree with coming clean, but I'm going to wait until next week when we're scheduled to meet."

"You're making a mistake, son."

"I've held off for months. What is a little over a week? She's been busy with work since she got back from visiting her family in Vegas for the holidays. Plus, she has a daughter to take care of, too. We're trying to finish the bikes for our current order before babies start dropping. And—"

"Stop," my dad said, effectively cutting me off. "You are making excuses to prolong the inevitable, which is new for you, because no matter what you did—right or wrong—you've never hidden behind excuses. The woman is going to be hurt by your actions. It's a given. What I want to know is where my son is? The son who has always known his own mind from the minute he could voice himself. The son who has always laid everything out, planned, then executed that plan to get what he wanted. Hell, it's what made you an outstanding SEAL."

"It's what I have been doing. I planned. I executed. I controlled the situation," I said, my voice raising with each statement, and stood. "But Gabriella still held back from me."

"You're a goner, and it has caused you to miss the obvious," my dad replied and followed up with a chuckle. He rose from the chair and moved until he stood in front of me. "What did you and the rest of your team do when a snafu occurred on one of your missions?"

"We stepped back, made adjustments to the plan."

"You adapted and executed under a new plan," he said, smiled, then turned and headed for the front door.

"Goddammit," was all I said.

"Life is one big ole mission. You plan and execute, and when a snafu happens, you adjust the plan. It's the difference between failing and succeeding. You might have started with one plan, but you didn't adjust it along the way. Really didn't matter, though. Your plan wasn't going to work because you forgot to account for the most vital part."

"Vital part?"

My dad opened the door and stopped before he stepped out onto the porch. "You were dealing with a woman," he said, walked out, and pulled the door closed behind him.

Fuck me. I thought I had control of the situation when, in fact, I had lost it the moment Gabriella had walked into my life. When it was all said and done, the only hope I had was that she felt half for me what I felt for her. I could work with that.

Gabriella

"Hello," I said as I swiped the screen on my cell without even looking at who was calling.

"I'm tired of waiting for you to call and I had a break between clients. Have you spoken to Max? Did you tell him?"

"I haven't had time, Tori. I've been working, like I am right now, and getting everything back on schedule from the holidays. Sawyer is adjusting to being back to school. We've had a lot going on."

"All excuses. Why are you dragging your feet?"

I sighed and stepped into the empty exam room. I didn't want to confess to my sister or myself, and I sure wasn't going to do it in the middle of a hallway at my place of business. "What if he doesn't feel the same, Tori? What if I confess I'm falling for him and he ends it because it's not what he's looking for?"

"Oh, honey, I don't think you need to worry about that. With everything you told me while you were here, he is in as deep as you. Come on, Brie, if it were only sex, nothing would have changed from the scheduled hookups. He was the one who initiated going out to dinner before going to the club or skipping the club altogether and taking you to a movie, a diner for coffee, and other places just to talk. Grabbing a drink and a hotdog from a street vendor while he walked with you on the pier. For God's sake, I say the man is not only in deep but that he is in love with you. Look at it this way, if Max turns out to be a grade-A asshole, you can always ask Sawyer to hook you up with Flirt. At least you know she likes him—maybe even has a little crush on him. And he must care enough for her because the biker boots and vest with interrogator on it was awesome."

"You don't think it was strange Flirt gave Sawyer a Christmas present?"

"Maybe a little at first, until I asked her about it. She told me how all the kids at Black Hawk have boots and a vest, and now she did, too. Maybe she said something about

114

it and, being a nice guy, he didn't want her to feel left out. Have you ever gotten the creepo vibe when you've been around any of the club members?"

"No, but he is the only one I haven't met."

"From what you say of the women and the men you have met; do you think they would let a perv or pedophile hang around?"

"No. They strike me as the type who would be more apt to kill him and hide the body," I said and chuckled.

"Listen, I need to get going, and you probably have a patient waiting. But, sis, go for it and tell the man how you feel. I think it might surprise you in the end. You deserve to be happy."

"I promise, I will. Don't work too hard."

"Love you, Brie."

"Love you, too, Tori."

I hit the button and disconnected. After a brief mental shake, I realized Tori was right, and I had nothing to lose. When Max and I meet up next week, I planned to lay it all out. It would either work or not. I'd deal with whatever happened.

Chapter Thirteen

Flirt

The wind hit me while I made my way to the hospital and held the bite of winter. With the official day of Spring still a couple months away, any break in the weather which allowed me to take my bike out was more than worth the cold air.

Slowing I turned into the hospital parking lot. Once I found an open spot for my bike, I parked and made my way to the entrance. Shortly the newest members of Black Hawk would make their appearance if they hadn't already.

As I rode the elevator to the maternity floor, I grinned, thinking not only of the call from Coast about Sami and Luna being in labor, which I received before I had reached the entrance to Whispering Nights. Turning around, I walked back to my and sat. I needed to send a text before I started my ride back home.

Unable to meet with u tonight. I will explain later. *G*—pinged my phone before I had finished typing out my message. I deleted what I had already written, then retyped a reply and hit send, *Hope everything is alright. Talk with u soon.*

Wouldn't she be surprised?

I was looking forward to seeing her since we hadn't been together since before Christmas. She and Sawyer had gone to Las Vegas to celebrate Christmas and New Year with her family. When she returned home, it was back to work, and this was the first time in the New Year we had a chance to get together.

Even though I missed and wanted to see her, there were many ways to do it without getting her upset. And she would be upset. I hadn't planned for it to happen that way today, but there was nothing I could do about it then.

The elevator stopped, and I stepped out. After looking at the sign on the wall with the arrow pointing in the direction of the waiting area, I headed down the hallway. I felt refreshed, happy, and content. The previous feeling of being out of sorts had long passed and was a distant memory as far as I was concerned. I chalked the brief period of doubt to the fact my best friends and brothers had each found women who fit them, which left me wondering if there was a woman made for me. And I was finally ready to admit, I had found her months ago. Admitting everything to my dad had helped bring it all into perspective.

I could admit I had felt left behind as my brothers started a different chapter in their lives, while my life felt as if it was at a standstill. At least until the last few months. Knowing it was in my head and not remotely true, I had concluded it had nothing to do with loneliness and everything to do with envy. I wanted a connection with a woman as they each had.

I felt it with Gabriella the moment I met her. There were just things we were going to have to work on before she was totally mine. First up—trust. Oh, she trusted me as a dominant to her submissive regarding what took place between us at Whispering Nights. She didn't trust me with anything outside of the club that didn't revolve around our sexual encounters. Even the time we had spent together outside the club, she'd held back only giving basic answers to questions about her life. If she only knew how out of character it was for me to take a woman on a date or spend time with one outside of sex—she would be shocked.

Though she'd shared her body with me a couple times a month, the only personal information she divulged was being a single mom with a little girl and generic information about her family. I had already deduced she had had a child from a couple of faint stretch marks marring the skin between her hipbones.

But it wasn't just Gabriella's silence when it came to personal information that irked a bit. When I had first met her, I did not know she lived in Shades Valley until I met Sawyer at Coast's house. The little girl's eyes were the same deep brown as her mother's. The resemblance between the two didn't stop there. They shared the same facial bone structure and the rich brown coloring of their hair.

For months, I kept the knowledge of Gabriella to myself and made sure I held parts of my life from her, too. Going as far as staying scarce when she was anywhere in the same area as me. Which was the opposite of how I was with her daughter. If Sawyer was at Sami and Speed's house, I would find myself drawn there. I enjoyed being around the kid. It had nothing to do with her being Gabriella's daughter and everything to do with I had fallen for a little girl, who was smart, funny, bold, and a little shy. I wondered more than once what traits came from her father. Sawyer's dad, yet another subject Gabriella never talked about.

She would be upset when everything was said and done, but I wouldn't allow her to stay mad at me for too

119

long. I couldn't. She was mine, and I was at the end of waiting for her to accept me and open up to me. I had fallen for her fast, and it was time she caught up. I needed her more than she would ever know.

I walked into the waiting room on the delivery floor and looked around. My brothers were there with their women and kids. Ally sat between Crusher and Carly, her legs swinging back and forth as she shifted in the chair.

"How long do babies take?" Ally asked Carly, making me grin.

"Well, some come quickly, and others take a while. It depends on how bad they want to come out and meet everyone," Carly answered her.

"Well, if they don't want to come out, why did they go in there in the first place, Dad?" Paxton looked up at Coast from his seat between him and his brother, Tracker. The look he gave my brother was one that said he trusted Coast as if he held the answer to everything.

I sat down beside my brother. "That's new," I commented as I nudged Coast's shoulder with mine.

Coast and Mac had filled out adoption papers almost immediately after they started fostering Tracker and Paxton. They had kept it from the boys, though. Coast hadn't wanted to jinx it. He had said that if they shared with the boys and then got denied; he feared it would set back the progress they were making with them.

Three weeks ago, right after the holidays were over, the call came through. Not only had they been cleared, but they had also been given a date for the four of them to appear before the judge to make it official.

In the courtroom we all sat and witnessed Coast and Mac legally become Tracker and Paxton's parents. The ICWA social worker from the reservation smiled and congratulated them. She'd been a tremendous supporter of the adoption of the two young boys.

It hadn't hurt either that the boys had thrived while living with Mac and Coast. Tracker's grades in school were excellent and above average. Paxton was also doing just as well in first grade. It had helped that he attended the same elementary school as Ally and where River taught.

"Yeah, it happened last week. No fanfare or anything. Saturday morning Paxton got up and came downstairs. Mac and I were in the kitchen, and he looked at Mac and asked, *What's for breakfast, Mommy?* She spilled her coffee all over the table, and while she was wiping it up, trying to hold herself together, Tracker walked in and asked, *What did you spill, Mom?* That did it, brother. She shoved the rag at me and told me to finish, then said she would be right back. I finished cleaning up, then got the cereal and milk out. Gave the boys each a bowl and spoon and then went to find her. She was in our bedroom crying her eyes out. By that evening, they were calling me dad. I am not ashamed to tell you a lump formed in my throat when they first said it. Best feeling, brother."

"I'm happy for you and glad everything is working out," I said and meant it. Coast was relaxed and no one looking at him or listening to him would miss the happiness on his face and in his voice.

"Thanks, brother."

"No thanks necessary. You deserve it. You chased the woman long enough," I teased and chuckled.

Coast snorted. "I had my doubts on more than one occasion whether I was going to catch her. It sank in at River and Jag's wedding after both you and Dad asked why I wasn't going after what I wanted. But I will be honest, I ended up with more than I ever thought I would or could have."

121

"I'm sure the others feel the same way with their women," I said and glanced around the room. No way my brothers knew when we came home from the military, their lives would change so drastically.

"Still can't believe Sami and Luna went into labor on the same day. This shit is crazy," Coast said and shook his head.

"It is. Was Mac worried about Luna being early?" I asked. Ghost had lost his first wife and son in a car accident while they were coming to meet him at the base after he and I and our SEAL team had come back from a mission. We left the military together, and he joined Black Hawk MC to work on healing after his loss. I had worried my friend would never make it back, but running into Luna had healed the last of his emotional scars.

"She told me on the way here that it isn't uncommon for twins to come early. She came in a bit ago and informed us both Sami and Luna were doing great. She said the twins were doing okay, and she didn't foresee an issue with Luna's or Sami's deliveries."

"Damn, I'm glad."

"Dad," Paxton said, and Coast looked over at the boy. "Yeah, Pax?"

"I asked why babies go in there if they don't want to come out?" Paxton asked again since Coast hadn't answered the first time.

I chuckled. "Yeah, why do they do it, brother?"

Coast turned his head back to me and glared. "Seriously?"

"You aren't going to be able to put it off much longer. Not with the way the women around here are dropping babies," I said and grinned.

One day at the shop Coast had shared with us that Paxton asked Mac how she gets the babies out of their mommies. She explained birth to a seven-year-old so he would understand, but when he followed up and asked how they got there in the first place, she distracted him with cake and told Coast that was his job to explain to Pax. It had been weeks, and evidently he still hadn't had the talk with Paxton.

"I'll get to it. Don't worry about it," Coast grumbled and turned back to Paxton.

"Mommies and daddies get together, and their love puts a baby in the mommy's belly," Ally piped in.

I knew then the conversation was going to take a turn for the worse. And no sooner than I had the thought—it happened.

"They don't have to love each other. He just has to stick his dic—" Coast shoved Tracker on the shoulder, cutting off the rest of his explanation.

"You complete that sentence and I'm going to take the Xbox," Coast said.

I put a fist to my mouth and feigned a cough to cover my laughter. Devil, Jag, and Crusher didn't even bother holding back their laughter.

River, who sat beside Jag with Poppy on his lap, rubbed her belly, then slapped Jag's arm. "You won't think it's funny when Poppy says stuff like that or our son," she pointed to her stomach.

Bailey looked at River from her spot. She sat on one side of Neely while Devil sat on the other side of the little girl. "I would reach over and smack Lance, but we all know the chance this one…" she rubbed her stomach, "after he is born, *not* saying or doing inappropriate things is a stretch, and we'd all be in denial if we thought differently." Every one of us laughed at Devil's expense as he glared at Bailey.

"When the babies get here, the boys are going to outnumber the girls five to three. Seven to three once River and Bailey deliver," I mentioned.

"That's cause girls rule, Uncle Flirt," Neely said.

"No, they don't," Paxton argued.

"Bailey said so, and she knows everything, and you don't," Neely argued back.

"Guys are always right," Tracker said backing Paxton up, which showed loyalty to his brother. But I shook my head and leaned back in the chair because Tracker was going to get a lesson in no good came from saying things like that to women. Even a small one.

"Are not!" Ally stood, and so did Neely. Poppy, barely over a year, clapped her hands and watched from Jag's lap as if cheering them on. That had to be a bad sign of what was to come when she got older.

"We're stronger and smarter, which makes us right," Tracker sneered, and Neely lunged. Devil grabbed the back of her shirt and it was the only thing that kept her from getting to Tracker. Neely was going to be a force to reckon with. The shy little girl Devil brought home had been replaced with one who showed no fear.

I glanced at Coast. "Brother, you going to step in?"

"He's going to have to learn sometime. It might as well be today. It will save him a shit ton of trouble with women when he's older."

"True."

"You didn't have to stop her. She is just a little girl. And I wouldn't hurt her," Tracker said as he looked at Devil.

Well, maybe it would take Tracker longer to learn.

Devil smiled. "Wasn't worried you'd hurt her, Trac. More worried about her hurting you." Tracker looked at Neely, and she grinned at him. The same shit-eatin' grin she shared with her brother. For the age gap between the half-siblings, they shared a lot of characteristics.

"Boys aren't smarter. They don't think with their brains. Aunt Carly says they think with their penises," Ally sneered at Tracker.

"Ally! You're not supposed to repeat what grownups say," Carly answered, affronted.

"Really, babe. You picked that to go with?" Crusher said to Carly and lifted a brow.

I leaned closer to Coast and lowered my voice, "You know, it's probably a good thing the boys are going to outnumber the girls. I have a feeling they're going to need those numbers to deal with them."

"I agree, brother. The teenage years on the compound won't be boring," Coast admitted.

"Our dads lived through it," I pointed out.

"Yeah, but there weren't any girls in the mix," Coast responded. I didn't have time to reply. Mac walked in, and the room went quiet.

She grinned. "Black Hawk MC has three new members. Archer Weston at eight pounds twelve ounces and twenty-two inches long. Lock Carver at six pounds two ounces and eighteen and a half inches long. Key Carver at six pounds and eighteen inches. Mothers and babies are doing great. Both dads stayed on their feet through it."

Everyone whooped and cheered, and I watched as Coast went and hugged Mac. When everyone settled down, Mac added. "After the parents and babies have a few minutes alone, you'll be able to go back. Ally, you get to come with me now to meet your brother."

Ally jumped from her seat and grabbed hold of the hand Mac held out. After they left, everyone started talking, and Crusher pulled out his phone and started texting. The dads had left that morning on a ride to Canada. When the women went into labor, they had turned around. The hospital would be the first place they stopped when they rode into town.

I leaned my head against the wall and watched my brothers interact with their families. We had been together since the day each of us was born. They were my club brothers, the brothers of my heart, and my best friends. I had witnessed each one fall when their woman entered their life. Leaving me the last man standing.

It wouldn't be for long if my plan worked.

We were talking when Mac walked in thirty minutes later and announced, "Sami and Luna are ready for visitors."

"We can split up. Half visits Sami, and the other half visits Luna, then we can swap," Carly suggested.

"If someone needs to stay here with the kids, I can. Then one of you can spot me after you have seen the babies," I volunteered, and it would allow me to put off the inevitable a while longer. Gabriella would arrive soon.

Mac looked over her shoulder into the hallway, then walked more into the room. "No one has to split up. Sami and Luna asked to share a room. So, they're in a semi-private. And as for the kids, well… they can visit, too."

"Look at you breaking the rules," Devil said.

"Stuff it, Dev. But if you get busted, I have no qualms throwing your asses under the bus and saying you snuck the kids in when I wasn't looking," Mac said matter-of-factly.

"Not sure that would work considering two of the kids are yours," I brought up, then stuck my hands up when Mac's head jerked in my direction and she glared at me.

"How come grownups get to break the rules, but when we do it, we get in trouble?" Paxton asked.

"Yeah!" Neely chimed in.

I snorted and received another glare, this time from Bailey. "What? At least they're in agreement. You should take it as a win." Bailey rolled her eyes, and I chuckled.

"Who's ready to see the babies? Sami and Luna are waiting to show them off," Mac said. Neely and Paxton jumped up. Paxton's question was forgotten, which was probably only temporary.

"She's good," I said only loud enough for Coast to hear.

"Geez, one of us needs to be. Mac is good at deflection. Comes in handy with Paxton's need for information," Coast said as we walked out of the waiting area and into the hallway. He and I brought up the rear of the group as we made our way to Sami and Luna's room.

"Damn, Tracker is going to be tall," I said when I noticed Tracker stood a good head taller than Mac while he walked beside her.

"Tell me about it. Already had to replace his jeans more than once."

"Was there a big adjustment going from living by yourself to an instant family of four?" I asked but didn't glance in Coast's direction. He and Mac made it look easy. Hell, all my brothers did.

"No. I wanted Mac and to make a family with her. Paxton and Tracker were a bonus for both of us since we can't have children. But you know what? Even if Mac and I could have kids, we would have taken in Paxton and Tracker. Honestly, in the short time they have been ours, I can't imagine not having them as our sons and part of the family." Coast's heartfelt words had me turning my head toward him. He shrugged. "When it's right, brother, you don't feel you've given up anything. But you sure as fuck are aware of everything you've gained."

Neither one of us said anything else as we approached Sami and Luna's room. We stopped as a group in front of the partially closed door. Mac pushed the door open and everyone filed in. As the last to enter the room, I stopped in my tracks at the sight before me.

Gabriella stood across the room with her head bent gazing down at the bundle of blue she held in her arms. I assumed it was one of Luna's and Ghost's sons since she was beside Luna's bed.

I hadn't expected her to beat me to the hospital. I had banked on it taking her longer because she wouldn't want to wear the outfit that she wore to Whispering Nights to the hospital, which would have meant a stop at her home.

When she sent me a text to cancel, I knew it was to go to the hospital. She'd gotten to know the women well even before we had gotten together. Especially since Sawyer was a friend of Ally's and the two little girls spent a lot of time together.

I also knew everything would be out in the open not only between us but with everyone. There was no way to avoid her here. I was surprised the secrecy had lasted as long as it had. She had no clue who I was. My only regret was I hadn't gotten to tell her beforehand, and now it would be like ripping a Band-Aid off... as everyone around us watched.

I rubbed the heel of my hand in the middle of my chest. If there had been a speck of doubt Gabriella wasn't meant to be mine, it'd disappeared when I spotted her cooing and swaying with the baby in her arms. It solidified she was the one I wanted everything with.

"No damn way. You and Brie?" Coast's voice jarred me out of my frozen state. His question and the nudge to my shoulder helped.

"What?" I looked over at him.

"You and Brie. How the hell have the two of you been able to keep this quiet?"

"Maybe because she doesn't know I'm a part of the Black Hawk MC." Later, I was sure I would laugh at Coast's wide-eyed reaction.

"How is that possible? She has been to dinner at Sami and Speed's house. Hell, she's been to mine and Mac's—" Coast stopped talking and stared at me. From his expression I could tell he was working on putting the pieces together. "You are never around when Brie is there. You always had some excuse. *'Going to work on the bikes a little longer.'* And you stay in the garage working while she is at Sami's. I invited you to dinner when Mac had her over, and you made some excuse about helping your dad. Why avoid her, brother? Why didn't you tell her?"

Thank God everyone else in the room was busy talking and gushing over the babies to notice or hear Coast and me.

"At first, I honestly didn't know who she was. It was only by chance we'd never run into each other around town or when she was at the compound. Once I figured out who she was... I was in too deep. Coast, I needed her to trust me with more than just her body. I was giving her the time to do that. I'll admit I've let everything go on too long. I was planning to tell her. Fuck, I'm an asshole. Even the day you all sent my dad by to check on me, he told me I messed up, and if I wanted a chance with her, I had better open up." I rubbed my fingers across my forehead.

What the fuck had I been thinking all this time? Time wasted. My need to be in charge and keep control had clouded my judgment. I couldn't lose her now.

"Christ, she was the one you were talking about the night I brought Mac to my house. You said you had found a new reason to keep going to Whispering Nights. For fuck's sake, the others and I have wondered what has been going on with you. We thought you were pulling away because you were feeling like the odd man out. Boy, were we wrong. Then the out-of-character outburst in the garage. Hell, we'd been right, it was because of a woman." Coast shook his head and then grinned.

"I'm not sure why you're grinning. Gabriella is going to be pissed once she notices me."

"Brother, pissed isn't going to come close. She's going to seem tame compared to our women." I frowned at Coast. "Oh, don't get that look. The women really like her, and they will be thrilled when Brie and Sawyer become officially part of the Black Hawk family... eventually. Maybe after they take a few layers of skin off you."

I shook my head and ran my hand across the back of my neck. "I might have miscalculated this situation."

"Ya think," Coast answered, then snickered. "Got any of those kink toys handy? Flogger, whip, crop, handcuffs, anything? It might be a good time to pull something out. This crowd could need restrained," he advised, and slapped my shoulder.

"You can be a dick," I said under my breath and turned my head to the suddenly quiet room. Which was shocking when I considered how many people were packed into the room. But what had my full attention was the dark brown eyes staring at me with flames shooting from them.

Yeah, I let the secrecy go on too long. And the sick part was I was actually turned on by the fire in her eyes and the mad radiating from her.

"Hey, Flirt. Get a look at the next generation," Ghost said, and my lips twitched when Luna slapped his arm and told him to hush. The brother would always have my back.

"Don't forget there are small ears in the room," Devil advised, his voice laced with humor.

"Be quiet, Lance," Bailey whispered, though in the quietness everyone heard her.

Ignoring Gabriella's death glare, I walked to the area between the two beds, stopped beside Sami's bed, and leaned down and kissed the top of her head. Then I moved to Luna's bed and did the same.

I looked between the two women and said, "You both look beautiful. No one would ever guess you two just delivered babies." I steeled myself and turned toward the woman who held my heart and my future in her hands. She could be mad and hurt as long as she needed to be—within a reasonable timeframe—I only had so much control when I wanted something.

"Gabriella."

Chapter Fourteen

Gabriella

A couple of miles from Whispering Nights, River called and informed me Sami and Luna went into labor. After pulling over, I texted Max to cancel our playtime. Which I would admit I'd gotten a bit upset when he answered back with a text that read as if he wasn't the least disappointed in the cancellation. I hadn't seen the man since well before Christmas. It didn't matter he had no clue I was going to confess to falling for him. Or that I wanted more with him than just being his submissive while hooking up at a kink club.

He could have at least added that he missed me to the text. The big jerk.

I turned my vehicle around and headed back toward Shades Valley, working to keep my focus on the road instead of obsessing over how he worded a text.

It was the man's fault. Max Browning made me feel things I had long since given up on experiencing again. If I were honest with myself, I would have admitted what I'd experienced with him to date was far beyond anything I could've imagined. That was yet another reason to push all thoughts of the man out of my head.

However, since the moment I had met him, he was never far from my thoughts.

When I reached town, I stopped at my place, and changed clothes. No way, I planned to show up at the hospital in a leather micro-mini skirt, a top that revealed an abundance of cleavage, and screamed 'look at my breasts.' Not to mention the leather ankle boots with spiked four-inch heels that finished my outfit off. I had been so damn excited to see him I had forgotten to throw my bag with spare clothes and an extra pair of comfortable shoes in my car.

At the house I changed into a sweater, jeans, and more comfortable boots, then went next door to check on Sawyer. Mrs. Grissom, who lived next door, was watching her. Before I could leave, it had taken the promise of as soon as they released the babies from the hospital and were home, I would take her to visit them. That and Mrs. G's mention of helping to bake cookies.

The drive to the local hospital hadn't taken long. Since I held privileges at the hospital, I pulled into an open spot in a section of the lot reserved for doctors. Once inside, I made my way through the hospital to the maternity ward nurses' station to check on Sami's and Luna's progress. When the nurse gave me a room number and told me the babies had already arrived, I was a slightly shocked. Not only about how fast the babies had made their appearance, but how long it had taken me to drive back to town, change clothes, check in on Sawyer and Mrs. G, and then make it to the hospital.

When I reached Luna and Sami's room, I knocked on the door, then pushed it open enough to stick my head in. Luna and Sami were sitting up in their beds. Ghost was leaning a hip on Luna's bed while Speed sat on Sami's. Ally stood between the beds looking into the hospital bassinets.

"Hey, up for a visitor?" I asked when heads turned toward the door.

"Of course. Come in, Brie," Luna said.

"You got here just in time before the room fills up. Mac went to the waiting room to let the gang know they could visit," Sami said.

I pushed the door open a little more and walked in, then partially closed the door again. Making my way between the beds, I stopped and looked down at the three little bundles. "Oh my God, look at those handsome little faces. Nice job, ladies."

"Uh, Ghost and I contributed, too." I chuckled at Speed's affronted tone.

"Why, yes, you did. How rude of me to not include you in a job well done."

"Thanks," both Ghost and Speed replied with big grins on their faces.

"Oh, yeah, they had a part. They got to…" Luna paused when Ghost coughed and lifted his chin toward Ally, "tickle their fancy and Sami and I ended up carrying the results, dealing with puking, heartburn, swollen feet, backaches, then pushing the fruit of their loins out of an area that defies nature by stretching to the size of a grapefruit," Luna said, making Sami and I laugh.

"What's tickle their fancy and fruit of their loins mean?" Ally asked as she joined Sami on the bed.

"Never mind what they mean," Sami said and kissed Ally on the top of her head.

"It means Luna sounds like an eighty-year-old woman for talking like that," Ghost said, then stepped back out of reach when Luna slapped at him. "You better behave, or I'm going to tell Ally how many curse words passed your lips in the delivery room."

"How many, Uncle Ghost?"

"If you tell, you'll never get the chance to talk me into having more kids," Luna said and laughed when Ghost glared at her.

"Daddy? Did my momma say any bad words?" Ally asked and looked at her dad. What I saw when Speed looked at Ally was a man who would never deny his daughter, even at the expense of having his significant other irritated with him.

Speed snorted, then grinned when Sami's head jerked in his direction.

"Kane, don't you dare," Sami said.

Even after getting to know and spend time with the women and men from Black Hawk, it still took me a second every time one of the men's given names was used versus their club names. It'd taken me quite a few times around the couples to realize the men's given names were only used by the women, and only when speaking of their own man.

"Would I rat you out, baby?" Speed asked and winked.

"I don't have to worry about getting ratted out. I didn't curse," Sami rebuked.

"Pretty sure, *I'm going to twist your damn balls off and shove them up your fucking ass,'* contains a few words that are construed as bad."

"Oh Momma," Ally said as she looked at Sami and shook her head.

I glanced at Luna and saw she had her face buried in Ghost's chest while her body shook. It took every ounce of my willpower not to burst out laughing.

One thing I quickly learned being around the group of men and women was I smiled and laughed a lot more.

"Why don't I take Ally to get a few snacks and some juice? With everyone here, I can watch the kids while the grownups are visiting," I said, hoping to distract Ally for Sami's sake.

"You don't have to do that. Mac's letting the kids come in since there are only three mothers on the floor right now. Us and one other lucky lady who spiced up her Friday, too," Luna said as she shifted around to adjust the pillow behind her back. It had fallen out of place when she had leaned forward to muffle her laughter.

"Can I hold Archer again before everyone comes in?"

"Let him sleep, baby. He can't be held all the time. It isn't good for him." Speed stretched his arm around Sami and between his response and the gentleness in the way he ran his hand down Ally's hair, had tears forming in my eyes on behalf of my daughter. Sawyer had never gotten the chance to experience being cherished by a dad's touch or words.

I remembered how it felt with my dad as a little girl and even still as an adult. Nero Agassi had never failed to show his two daughters, Victoria and myself, that he loved us. If I closed my eyes, I could even picture him doing it. He had even done the same thing to my brother Enzo, at least until he reached his teen years and decided it was embarrassing to have your dad hugging you. Well, at least while other were around to witness it.

When Sawyer and I had lived close to family, my dad had done the same with her, but nothing replaced the touch from a dad or the bond between a little girl and her father. Not even a grandpa's touch.

One twin wiggled, then whimpered, and it brought me back to where I was. "Can I hold him?" I asked Luna.

"Of course. That one is Lock," she said, then chuckled. "I think. We might have to put different color wristbands on them until we can tell them apart."

I picked the baby up, opened the blanket until I could read the hospital wristband. I looked at Lock's face, then down at Key as I fixed Lock's blanket back into place. "Yeah, good luck with that." Not a single difference showed in their tiny faces.

"Thanks. Your doctor's knowledge of children is shining bright," Luna said sarcastically.

I chuckled, and the movement of my chest with the sound made Lock squirm in my arms.

"Sorry, little man," I said as I swayed side to side to settle him down. "I think they favor Ghost. At least for now. They change so fast. Who knows what they'll look like in three months."

"They'll still look like Brax. Under their hats is his dark brown hair. I don't see it switching to blonde. Maybe I will get lucky with their eyes, but somehow I doubt it. They'll probably end up with his gray ones, too."

"Archer looks like my momma," Ally said and slid off Sami's bed so she could get a better look at her brother. "I guess that's fair since Aunt Carly said I look so much like my daddy, I could have popped out his butt." Speed snorted, and Sami closed her eyes and sighed. Before anyone could say anything else, the door was pushed open, and Mac entered with the rest of the group following behind.

I moved around to the other side of Luna's bed to get out of the way. When the ooh's and aah's started, the sound in the room rose a few decibels. Lock squirmed in my arms, and Key and Archer stirred in their beds. Which wasn't a huge deal since there were women who were dying to get a hold of them.

I smiled at Lock while I swayed back and forth with him. Holding him in my arms brought back memories of Sawyer as a baby. It had been a happy time and one of great sadness for me. Pushing that thought away, not wanting to travel down the road of my past in a room full of people, I placed my focus on Lock. I cooed and murmured to him while I listened to the others in the room. I knew the quieter I stayed, the longer I would get to hold him before someone stole him away.

There must have been five different conversations going on in the room. It happened a lot when this group was together. I had stopped paying attention to what everyone was saying when a familiar voice broke through and registered.

"I might have miscalculated this situation."

I scanned the room until my eyes landed on the man the voice belonged to. He ran his hand across the back of his neck as he shook his head. Unaware I was staring at him.

I assumed he was talking to Coast because he stood beside him. Coast confirmed it when he answered with, "Ya think?"

Coast looked in my direction, then to my shock, said in not so quiet voice, "Got any of those kink toys handy? Flogger, whip, crop, handcuffs, anything? It might be a good time to pull something out. This crowd could need restrained," then Coast slapped Max's shoulder.

I didn't hear "dick" as much as I read it on Max's lips. I also realized I was not the only one who heard them because the room had gone quiet.

Awesome.

Frozen in my spot, at first wondering what Max was doing here before it struck me. He was the elusive Flirt everyone, including my daughter, spoke of, but I had yet to meet. There was always a reason for his absence when the other men had been around. If I thought of at all the times he was conveniently missing, it made sense. Avoidance. He purposely kept the information away from me.

"Hey, Flirt. Come get a look at the newest members," Ghost said, verifying I was correct.

I heard Luna hush him, but I didn't glance toward her. Everything was running through my head at once. Did everyone know? How much did they know? I felt betrayed, and as I thought about what a fool I'd been made of, anger set in. How dare him or them?

"Don't forget the small ears in the room," Devil said.

Ah, yes. I had briefly forgotten about Ally, Neely, Paxton, and Tracker being in the room.

"Be quiet, Lance," came from Bailey. And as usual, it took a second to link Lance with his club name, Devil. Geez, how did the women keep track?

Max was the first to break eye contact between us, and I watched as he walked between the two beds. He stopped beside Sami's bed and leaned down and kissed the top of her head, then he moved to Luna's bed and kissed the top of her head, too.

He looked between the two women and spoke with ease as if there wasn't now a colossal elephant in the room. "You both look beautiful. No one would ever guess you just delivered babies." Then he turned to face me. "Gabriella," came smoothly from his lips as if there weren't over a dozen people's eyes focused on us.

I leaned down and kissed Lock on the forehead, then held him out to his mother.

"Brie," was all Luna got out before I shook my head, cutting off whatever she planned to say.

"Thanks for letting me hold him." She sighed and took her son from my arms. "I'll be back mid-afternoon to do the circumcisions," I said, glancing between Luna and

Sami. I forced myself to include the others. "I appreciate you letting me share this special moment with you."

The others moved and gave me room to pass. When I felt a hand touch my arm, I didn't even turn my head. "Don't touch me," I said, my voice slightly cracking.

The hand dropped away, and Max said, "You have to let me explain."

"That would be great if I actually cared enough to listen to you, which I don't." I walked to the door, pulled it open, and headed toward the bank of elevators. Hopefully, I would hold it together long enough to make it to my car. It wouldn't take much more to have tears flowing.

One set of elevator doors slid open, and I stepped in not even looking to see if it was going up or down. All I thought was, *not much longer,* as the doors closed. When a hand appeared and stopped the progress, I briefly forgot about the tears I was holding off. "Do not get on this elevator. I don't want to talk. I don't want to listen. Damn it, I don't want to look at you right now. And lastly, I don't want to make a scene, but I will if I'm left no choice." My voice broke at the end, and whatever he had planned to say to me, he kept to himself. With one last look into my eyes, Max stepped back and let the doors close.

Thankful the elevator had been on its way down, I hurried out when the doors opened and exited the hospital in anticipation of reaching my car before I broke down. Instead, it seemed life wasn't quite done with me for the day.

"Hey, I've been thinking of you and here you are," Dr. Chad Booker, aka the doctor every woman wanted, at least by his account, said as soon as I made it to the sidewalk.

Ugh, I was so close to escaping. And so not in the mood to deal with him. I had met my quota of the day dealing with assholes.

"Well, nice running into you…" *NOT* "but I'm in a hurry," I said, and he grabbed my arm as I tried to step around him.

"Your practice must really keep you busy. I've even tried to get in touch with you several times by phone. You're not picking up or returning my calls."

I looked down at the hand that still held my arm, then back at him. "Yeah, I'm pretty sure fifty-plus calls isn't remotely close to several times, Chad. Now let go of my arm, I need to go, and I'm sure there are patients in the ER waiting to be seen."

The phone calls I received from him probably numbered closer to a hundred. After listening to the first five voicemail messages, I just started deleting the other messages he'd left without listening.

We'd had one date over six months ago for God's sake. It had been two hours across a dinner table and more than enough time for me to realize I wasn't interested in a second date. Heck, there wouldn't have been the first date if I'd had any inkling of his reputation prior. I figured by now he had run out of female nurses and doctors to hit on, at least until the hospital hired new ones.

"I wouldn't have to keep calling if you'd quit playing hard to get, Brie. It's getting exhausting."

What the hell? Talk about exhausting. And where were the people who were constantly milling about outside the hospital? It seemed as if I couldn't catch even a tiny break.

I hated being rude or mean. Sometimes, though, it was the only way to get through to certain people.

"Since you didn't take my nonresponse as I'm not interested, let me see if I can put it plainly enough for you to understand. I am not interested in you, Chad. Stop calling because you are wasting your time if you think I will change

142

my mind. There'll be no more dinner dates... nothing. I don't even want to stand here and talk with you. Buy a vowel or get a clue, whichever you want. But I am done. D.O.N.E. Now, release my arm and step the fuck away."

"You are gonna want to listen to the lady." Chad's hand dropped away as I swung my head around to see who had spoken.

I had definitely been focused on dealing with Chad because I hadn't heard the men approach us. I felt a marginal amount of relief when I recognized them. I had been introduced to them when I had been at the Black Hawk's compound, and they'd stopped by Sami's house looking for Speed and the others. Even knowing their names—their club names anyway—I couldn't remember which dad belonged to which man.

"Dr. Agassi and I are having a private conversation. It isn't any of your concern," Chad replied in a superior tone. One I heard throughout our dinner together and part of the reason for my lack of interest in having any further personal interaction with him. There wasn't much I could do about it professionally since I held privileges at the same hospital, and frequently we ran into each other if I was on call in the ER.

I watched one side curve up on the man's mouth who stood in front of the others. "You made it our concern when you didn't remove your hand right away when the lady asked. We also heard her tell you to step the fuck away," he replied, then glanced at me. "Brie, right?" I nodded, and he asked, "Are you coming or going?"

"I was on my way home."

"I'll walk you to your car, honey," one of the other men volunteered.

"You know these... men?" Chad asked, and I didn't have to look at him to know his face was more than likely distorted to match the disgust his tone carried.

"Yes, I do," I answered with no intention of telling Chad I didn't know the men well. Instead, I shifted my eyes and answered the man who had spoken last, "I would appreciate the escort to my car."

"We'll finish our conversation another time, Brie," Chad said, glared at me, then turned toward the entrance.

"Not if I can help it," I replied and got the satisfaction of watching Chad storm through the doors as they slid open.

The men laughed as the one who offered to walk me to my car stepped forward and placed his hand on the small of my back.

"I won't be but a few minutes, brothers," he said to the others as he led me to the edge of the sidewalk and we stepped off onto the pavement.

"We'll meet you at the elevator, Romeo. Probably be a good idea to swing by the gift store if it is open and snag something for Sami and Luna," another of the men said, then the four turned and walked inside.

"I'm sorry for holding you up. Please, you don't need to walk me to my car. Go see the babies," I rushed on, feeling a little embarrassed since Chad went inside, and I had a few seconds to digest everything that had happened. To include what these men must think of me after the little episode they witnessed. As if I hadn't already been humiliated once today. Now it seemed I was two for two.

"The babies aren't going anywhere. Where did you park, honey?" the man beside me asked as we headed toward the parking lot.

I sighed. "It's over there," I said and pointed.

"Does Doctor Dickhead harass you often?" he questioned.

I gave an unladylike snort at the name Chad would forever be labeled in my head. "No. He just has a problem accepting that not all women drop at his feet," I said as I reached in my pocket and pulled out my keys. I hit the button on the key fob and unlocked the doors as we reached my car. "Thank you for the escort... Uh, I'm sorry. I remember the names from Sami's introduction, just not which one goes to whom."

"Romeo," he answered, smiled, and opened the driver's side door for me.

"Well, thank you for the escort, Romeo," I said, and returned his smile with one of my own.

"Never need to be thanked for an opportunity to walk a beautiful woman to her car," he said and winked, then he frowned. "Which has me wondering why my son didn't walk you out of the hospital. I am assuming you were visiting Sami and Luna, right? I am glad Flirt finally came clean with you, and you didn't hold his stupidity against him."

"Yes," I answered as I eased into the driver's seat of my car. Then everything he said registered. I pinched the bridge of my nose instead of following through with the initial urge of banging my head on the steering wheel. How distraught I'd been, between the disappointment in Max and then the run-in with Chad, that it hadn't registered one of the older men was Max's dad.

Sami had told me after introducing the five older men that they were mostly referred to as *the dads*. It was also when I learned there had originally been six of them who started the Black Hawk MC. However, Speed and Carly's dad had died in a motorcycle accident caused by a man Carly had thought was her real dad at the time. Their entire story had reminded me of a book. Then, over my time spent with the women, they each had shared how they had met their other half as we'd gotten to know each other better.

God, they had mentioned Flirt a hundred times. Didn't anyone use real damn names? If they had called him Max just one time, it would have clicked, or I would have

145

maybe questioned the coincidence. Even joked about knowing two Maxes. No, I refused to put any blame on my friends. This whole situation was Max's fault for not being upfront from the beginning. The women had to have been as shocked as I was, which made me feel a little better. And how could I blame them? It wasn't as if I'd mentioned Max by name around them either. The most they knew was that I was a member of a BDSM club, and I went twice a month. I hadn't even shared the name of the club, even with Carly badgering.

"Are you okay, sugar?" Romeo's question brought me out of my head. Though it seemed while Max had hidden information from his friends, he had shared it with his dad.

I let go of the bridge of my nose and looked at the man who still held onto my car door. "You really have to look closely, but the resemblance is there. He has your jawline, nose, and the shape of your eyes. Are you an asshole, too?"

His lips twitched, and he rubbed his chin between his thumb and fingers. "Guess it would depend on who you ask, honey."

There was so much I wanted to say and ask the man, but honestly, I was just done. Max was a grown man, and Romeo wasn't responsible for his son's idiocy.

"At least you're honest. Maybe you can give your son some pointers on that," I said, and reached for the door handle. "Thanks again." I pulled and hoped he would let go of the door. I wanted to leave and put an end to the day.

"He should have been honest with you from the beginning. I told him as much when we talked last. But, Brie, Flirt's—"

"I don't need or want to hear anything about your son. He had months to explain or come clean, as you said. Instead, he waits until I am in a room full of people I think of as friends. Your son is an asshole. Now please let go of my door. I have a daughter I need to get home to, and I have lost the last of my patience with men today. Doctors and bikers are at the top of the list." I pulled on the handle again, and Romeo let go and stepped back. With the door shut, I started my car and backed out of the parking spot. I didn't look in the rearview mirror to see if he stood in the same spot or not.

I drove home. Parked and turned the keys to the off position. Rested my forehead against my hands that still gripped the wheel, then let the frustration, humiliation, and angry tears flow.

I promised myself they would be the only tears shed over Max "Flirt" Browning.

Chapter Fifteen

Flirt

The weight of how I handled everything settled on my shoulders as the elevator doors closed. The devastation in Gabriella's eyes was crippling. My need for control—control I needed to keep my life balanced—seemed inconsequential at the moment. I felt as though I had lost everything and for the first time unsure how to go about getting my life back on track.

I thought about taking the stairs and getting on my bike and riding until my head cleared, then going home. It would have kept me from facing everyone in the room, but I couldn't do it. They were my family. I would take what they dished out because I deserved it.

Turning to head back toward the room, I noticed Mac, with Poppy on her hip, and the other kids walking toward me. If the other women's expressions were anything like Mac's, they were going to chew my ass or skin me alive.

Mac never said a word. She just pushed the down button for the elevator and faced the doors as she waited.

Tracker, Paxton, and Neely glanced at me with looks of pity but said nothing. Ally had no problem tossing her opinion toward me.

"You're in big trouble. You hurt Sawyer's momma's feelings. Are you going to fix it?"

"I'll try."

Ally sighed, "Uncle Flirt, you have to do more than try."

"It's all I'm able to promise right now, Ally. Sawyer's momma is pretty upset with me… among others," I tacked on.

"Okay, but sometimes if you say you're sorry, ya don't get into much trouble. They just tell ya not to do it again," Ally said and pursed her lip before adding. "If you cry a little that helps, too."

"I'll take that into consideration. Thanks for the advice," I answered, and Mac snorted.

Who could blame Mac? I stood in the hospital's hallway listening to the advice of a little girl. If I weren't the one who caused the mess, I would have found humor in the situation, too.

It saved me from more humiliation when the elevator stopped, and the doors opened. As Mac and the kids got on the elevator, I walked back to the room. With one hand on the door I used my other and swiped down my face, then took a deep breath, blew it out, and pushed the door open. By the looks on everyone's faces, Ally was right—I was in big trouble.

"I'm sorry. Bad judgment call on my part," I said as I stepped fully into the room. Yeah, how ironic I used Ally's advice, but I would be damned if I added tears. "And I apologize for ruining a happy day with my bullshit. I knew Gabriella would stop by and I should have stayed away until she left."

"Brother, what the ever-loving fuck was that?" Speed was the first to speak.

"I imagine it's what a train wreck looks like," Devil responded.

"Maybe if everyone onboard caught on fire," Jag added.

"Brutal was what it was," Crusher piped in.

I looked between Coast and Ghost and held my hands out, palms up. "Anything you want to add?"

"No, I contributed enough with my teasing words, which I'm sure I'll hear about later from Mac," Coast said.

Ghost laid the son he held in his arms down, then rested a hip on the side of Luna's bed before he spoke. "You and I have been through a lot together. We have a bond as SEALs that has grown even more since I came home with you and joined the MC. You've never once wavered in supporting me, and you know I will always have your back regardless of what is going on. I could tell you how wrong today was, but you know that already. I received a second chance at a family and life because you and the others in this room wouldn't let me give up on myself. Brother, I want to return the favor. You lectured each of us on grabbing what we wanted and not settling for less. You have told us more than once exactly what you would do if you found the perfect woman.

"And though what happened here was dreadful, I honestly don't believe you set out to hurt Brie. So, if she is your woman, I'll do whatever I can to help you fix this fuckup. You deserve to be as happy as we are."

When Speed, Crusher, Devil, Coast, and Jag each agreed with Ghost, I had to swallow to remove the lump that had formed in my throat. But I was under no delusion the women were going to be as generous. Especially when not one of them had spoken since I returned.

I ran my hand across the back of my neck. If I couldn't be honest with family, who could I be honest with? And everyone in the room was my family.

The simple fact was I had known the minute Gabriella walked through the door at Whispering Nights she was mine. Each time we were together only solidified it more for me. I looked around the room before I responded, "I might have let this situation go on too long and bruised Gabriella's feelings. She'll get over it because I refuse to allow it to go any other way. I will do what is necessary to remedy the problem. Gabriella *is* mine, and I will make her see it." My brothers grinned at me while each woman's face wore a different expression.

Luna jumped in first. "Brie will either fall into your arms or rip your balls off."

"I'll take 'rip your balls off' for twenty," came from Carly.

"Of course, you always choose the violent way to go," Sami said to Carly, then she looked in my direction. "I have gotten to know Brie pretty well since Ally and Sawyer became friends. I don't know why you felt the need to keep your association with Black Hawk from her, and honestly, it's the least important part of this. But I know you, Flirt, and I believe the reason is important to you. However, misguided we think it is. Though it has to be more than just your need…" Sami paused as if drawing a blank on what to say, which gave the others a chance to jump in and come to her aid.

All four women spoke simultaneously.

"For kinky sex," Luna prodded.

"To get his freak on," came from Carly.

"To dominate someone," came from River.

"To have controlling sex," came from Bailey.

Christ and not one woman had a clue about a D/s relationship. I looked at each of my brothers and lifted a brow. They shrugged and smirked. If the bastards thought I would do any explaining, they were crazy. They could answer their own woman's questions.

Sami shook her head at the women and sighed. "No, I was trying to think of a nicer way of saying 'his need to be a controlling jerk' not just dealing with sex," Sami said, then elbowed Speed, who snorted while he sat beside her on the bed. Her eyes softened when she looked back at me. "Like I mentioned before, I have gotten to know Brie pretty well. We all have. I will mention nothing we've discussed. I just want you to know she is our friend, at least she was before today. What happened here was unnecessary and I don't want to see her hurt again like that. Brie is a strong and sweet woman who loves her job and her daughter. She is settling in here and I don't want to see her give up everything and move. It took guts to move away from family to a town where you didn't know one person. At least when Dad moved Carly and me here, we had each other."

"Sami, for fuck's sake, I don't want to hurt her either. I also would never ask what Brie has said around you. But if there is something I need to know about her or Sawyer that could affect their wellbeing, then I would expect to be told," I said and immediately regretted the bite in my tone. Speed's lifted brow and curled lip let me know he wasn't going to accept it from me, either. Especially when aimed toward his ol' lady.

Sami touched Speed's forearm as she answered me, "There is nothing we know about her you couldn't have learned if you had tried to get to know her. If Brie is yours, as you so cavemanishly put it, maybe you should ask yourself why she doesn't talk to you? You have been seeing her for months, Flirt. I thought the whole thing with a D/s

153

relationship was getting to know and understand each other on *all* levels. Not just sex. Why haven't you done your job as a Dom, Flirt? Why hasn't Brie felt as if she could share anything about herself outside of the two of you getting off?"

Damn if I didn't feel that verbal slap.

"Christ, Sami, what happened to putting things nicely?" Speed asked.

"I guess you and Carly are rubbing off on me," Sami said and shrugged.

"Sex is the easy part," River spoke while I was still running everything over in my head that Sami said.

"Opening yourself up is the hard part because once you have, the person then has the ability to hurt you," Bailey added.

"Of course, it's hard. No one wants to open up and share the crazy shit or show any vulnerability," Carly jumped in.

"Sometimes it's their flaws they don't want to share," Luna said.

"Please, I have no flaws," Devil voiced and then grinned when every head in the room jerked in his direction.

Bailey groaned, then rubbed her hand over her extended belly. "I'm probably going to be committed after Neely and this one gets through their teen years."

"No sense stressing over it now. Besides, it is too late; you are stuck with us. Just be comforted in knowing I will spare no expense on a place to care for you," Devil said. He wasn't quick enough on his feet to move out of Bailey's reach when her arm swung out and the back of her hand connected with his stomach.

"We were right that day at the garage. It was a woman who had you in a foul mood. Brie's the reason for that mood and why you have been ducking out and hiding when we get together, right? And not anything to do with you pulling away because you feel you don't fit in since we have families? Cause if the latter is the case, you are a fucking dumbass," Ghost said, and everyone's eyes came back to me.

"Well, that was subtle," Luna said to Ghost, who shrugged. My friend and I had been through a lot together as SEALs. Team members share a bond, not unlike an MC. Loyalty and trust in each other are paramount. Out of all the men in the room, he probably knew me best, which considering I grew up with the others said a lot.

"Yes, I was ducking out because of Gabriella. And no, I am not a dumbass. I might be envious of what all of you have found, but I wasn't pulling away from you. You're my family. For the record I was going to come clean to her today, but the babies took that out of my hands," I said and sighed.

"You could have what we've found with Brie. You know that, right?" Coast said, and when I looked in his direction, he added. "What Ghost said deserves repeating. You had plenty to say to each one of us, so I am going to give it right back to you. Where is the man who said if he found the right woman he would tie her to his bed until she understood she was his?"

"I'm going to add I have never known you to hold back on anything you've wanted. Honestly, brother. How can you be upset about Brie not trusting you? How do you think she feels that not only didn't you share anything about yourself—you ran for cover whenever she was around? Trust works both ways, brother," Ghost said, calling me out.

"I get it," I answered. "I couldn't have fucked things up more, even if I had tried."

Nobody responded because the door opened, revealing Mac and the kids were back. Evidently, they ran into the dads somewhere along the way since they brought up the rear. At least their return halted any more talk on the disaster of my making.

As everyone moved into the room, I wasn't sure if we were all going to fit, so I decided to lessen the crowd by one. After digesting what Sami and Ghost said, it brought home exactly how badly I had messed up with Gabriella and lifted my desire to make it right. It was a first for me where a woman was concerned. Usually, it never bothered me if a female got her feathers ruffled. Gabriella upset, though, didn't sit well with me.

"Ran into your woman outside. Fucked up good, did you? I got the impression she was more than upset," my dad said as he walked up beside me and slapped me on the back.

"Yes, I had it planned, and it fell through… Hell, I got no excuse," I admitted. At least I didn't have to go over what had taken place a hundred times. It seemed the entire club was now aware of the drastic turn my life took inside of a couple of hours and the stupidity that had led to it. It had to be a record. The internet had nothing compared to the club's capability to pass information. "I'm going to repair the damage as soon as I leave here." I wasn't going to waste time riding around to clear my head, and I wasn't going to put off righting my wrong until tomorrow. I'd hurt Gabriella by not sharing exactly who I was—she would soon meet the real me.

"Hope it includes some groveling," he said and smirked.

"I don't grovel. Anyway, how do you know I did anything wrong to make her upset? You just rode into town."

"Ha! You boys should know from experience that nothing happens we don't hear about. Besides, I ran into Brie outside. When a woman has her back up that much, a man is the cause. Brie has some fire in her, too." I heard the respect in my dad's voice.

"I know she does. But that's no cause to grovel."

"There're different ways of groveling, son. Not all involve a man crawling or kowtowing to get what he wants. Just like plowing forward or strong-arming doesn't always bring results. You have always regulated every aspect of your life, Flirt. Relaxing a little could be a good thing. Now go work on getting your woman. You can't give them time to let things fester, and from what I observed, she was more than halfway there. Of course, the asshole doctor harassing her probably didn't help either," my dad said as he took a step in the direction where the other dads stood inspecting the newest members.

"What asshole doctor?" I asked, getting my own back up. Which hadn't taken long since I was already working toward a good mad. The difference was the growing mad was my fault. Nothing would please me more than to turn it on someone else.

"Nametag said, Dr. Booker. We walked up on the altercation. What I heard and could make out is he has been calling and leaving messages and isn't too happy Brie is ignoring him."

"Is he harassing her?" I asked, unsure I wanted the answer because I would have liked nothing better than to take my frustrations out on the doctor.

"He wasn't happy with us interrupting, but Brie was holding her own. He strikes me as the type of man who doesn't take rejection well." Dad's expression showed he didn't care for the man's attitude.

"I'll handle the good doctor if I need to," I said and turned toward the door.

"I don't think he'll be a problem. She pretty much put him in his place. You need to worry more about fixing your problem with Brie than the doctor." I glared over my shoulder and my dad smiled. "I look forward to welcoming a daughter-in-law and granddaughter into the family soon. Seems my son finally pulled his head out of his ass."

"Even so, it could still take a while," I answered as I reached for the door handle.

"My money is on you. Never seen you fail when you wanted something bad enough. Can't imagine you'd start now."

I shook my head. "Yeah, but I have never fucked something up this bad before." I pulled the door open and walked out of the room. My dad's words about being ready to welcome Gabriella and Sawyer into the family were pretty much his stamp of approval. His last statement, though, was a direct hit. He was right—I had never failed when something mattered to me. Gabriella and Sawyer definitely fit into that category.

Chapter Sixteen

Gabriella

"I can't wait to see the babies. Maybe Sami and Luna will let me hold one of them. Do you think they will? Did Ally get to hold her brother? I wish we had a baby. I would hold it all the time. I'd be the bestest sister. Can you have another baby for us?" Sawyer had been talking nonstop in her quest to know everything about the babies since I picked her up at Eleanor's house. It at least kept her from noticing my swollen eyes and the splotchy skin on my face. The result of crying the entire way home from the hospital and more than a couple splashes of cold water could fix.

The tears had flowed down my cheeks the entire way home. By the time I parked my car in the garage, I was drained mentally and physically. I couldn't recall ever experiencing every emotion imaginable in such a small space in time—shock, anger, annoyance, betrayal, sadness. After I went inside the house I blew my nose, splashed cold water on my face, and prayed I could keep it together long enough to collect Sawyer. Eleanor wasn't as easily fooled, and when she stared at my face and lifted a brow, I gave a shake of my head. Thankfully, she took the hint and hadn't asked any questions in front of Sawyer.

Once Sawyer and I were home, I held my emotions in check and went through our evening ritual. After a snack and Sawyer dressed for bed, though still going full steam ahead, she was blissfully unaware I was hanging on by a thread. I only needed to get her into bed, then I would spend some quiet time and wallow. I would get everything out of my system to include Max Browning.

I tucked the blanket around Sawyer and planted a kiss on her forehead. "Love you, sweetie."

"You didn't answer my questions," Sawyer said instead of responding with her usual 'love you more.'

"What questions?" I asked, realizing I had been inside my head rather than listening to my daughter.

"Do you think Sami and Luna will let me hold the babies? Ally probably got to hold her brother."

"I'm not sure, sweetie. That is up to Sami and Luna, but if they do, you have to be super careful with the babies."

"Did Ally get to hold him?" The child was relentless.

"She did, but I'm sure it was under the watchful eye of her mother."

"Can you have a baby for us? I'd be the bestest sister. I'd hold it even when it cried. And feed it."

"Whoa, sweetie." For the first time since I left the hospital I smiled without having to force it. "I know you would be an awesome sister and very helpful, but that's not a good reason to have a baby."

"Okay," Sawyer said with a sigh, then yawned.

"Go to sleep, sweetie, and I promise to take you to see the babies as soon as Sami and Luna are home with them."

"I wish I could go to the hospital with you tomorrow," she said as she snuggled under her covers.

"I'm not visiting tomorrow, sweetie. I told you I was going because I'm the babies' doctor. Trust me, they aren't going to be in a good mood after I see them, and they are going to want their mommies."

"I know. They got to get the boy proceeds done," she huffed, and I tried not to chuckle at her mispronunciation.

"Yes, the procedure. They are getting circumcised," I corrected and reached for the bedside lamp.

"Glad I don't got a penis," she said and rolled onto her side and closed her eyes. My girl was too smart for her own good. Sawyer had asked questions from the time she could talk.

I turned the lamp off, leaving her room in the soft glow of the nightlight, and walked out. After a stop in my room to change into a pair of sleeping pants and tank top, I made my way barefoot through the quiet house. After a quick stop in the kitchen for a glass of wine, I ended up on a corner of the couch with my legs tucked under me. I took a healthy gulp, then set the glass on the table, and gave into the emotions I had been holding at bay. As the tears flowed, I was struck with the strongest of feelings—loss. The loss of what Max and I shared. The loss of what was growing between us. And the loss of the piece of my heart Max already held.

The tears slowed, and the anger set in along with the question—Why? Why keep his identity from me? I thought with the time we spent together outside of Whispering Nights, we were building more of a connection than just sexual partners. I thought maybe we were falling in love.

While I wondered what bothered me more—the embarrassment in how I found out or the hurt of thinking I meant so little to him. I rested my head against the couch cushion, closed my eyes, and let the exhaustion pull me under.

My eyes popped open, and I jerked my head upward, which caused me to slap my hand on my neck as pain radiated because of the fast movement. The pain resulted from the stiffness in my neck, stemming from dosing off in an awkward position. I hadn't had to wait long to figure out what startled me awake—knocking at the door.

I stood, rubbed my neck, then walked to the door. I don't know why I bothered looking out the peephole when I knew who would be on the other side. Standing at the door, I debated yelling for him to leave before the adult in me kicked in. It had turned out to be a craptastic evening, so why not deal with it face to face and be done?

"Gabriella, open the door. I know you're standing on the other side. You need to let me in. I am not going to leave until we talk." At Max's words, I squinted my eyes and glared at the door. Seriously? No, *sorry*. No, *I have been a complete ass*. Not even a simple, *please* while asking to be let in.

I flipped the deadbolt and the flimsy lock on the doorhandle in one move while using both hands, then swung the door open. "How did I not realize you are a bossy buffoon with no manners?" I spouted and the slight twitching of his lips did nothing to calm the anger brewing inside me. Anger, I could deal with. It beat the hell out of crying and berating myself for being stupid.

When Max didn't respond to my snarky-ness, I stepped back and allowed him to enter. After he walked in, I closed the door, inhaled deeply, and blew the breath out before I turned around to face him.

"You can take a seat in the living room," I waved toward the room, "while I check on Sawyer to make sure she is still asleep." I didn't wait for him to reply.

At Sawyer's door, I peeked in, and after verifying she wasn't faking, I pulled the door closed. When I reached the living room, Max stood at the table that showcased various framed pictures in assorted sizes.

"This is you at around Sawyer's age, isn't it?" he questioned and moved to the side so I could see which picture he was pointing at.

"Yes," I replied as I moved further into the room.

"Christ, I knew the resemblance was strong, but looking at these pictures side by side—she's your doppelgänger. Now I am questioning why it took me a minute to place her as your daughter," he stated, then shook his head and turned around to face me. "I met her the day after our first... physical encounter at Whispering Nights. She fired questions at me, then informed me you were single, too." Max chuckled.

"Yes, Sawyer is always full of questions. Which isn't a bad thing. She just hasn't learned the difference between what is intrusive and what's construed as being an inquisitive little girl," I said, then continued to stand in the middle of the room at a loss for what to say next. It was Max who was set on getting it all out. He wanted to explain, then he could get on with it. And if he was waiting for me to ease his conscience, it was going to be one long ass wait for him.

"I'm sorry I hurt you. I wouldn't have if I had been honest from the start." He closed the gap between us until he stood in front of me. Close enough, I could see the regret in his eyes.

"Yes, I believe you are. I won't lie, it hurt and embarrassed me. But also confused me. When you found out who I was, why didn't you mention it to me? I realize Whispering Nights leaves it up to their members to share personal information outside of health issues, of course, with whomever they have partnered with. However, I'd wager there have been members who have run into other members outside of the club at some point. So why not come clean? I mean, big deal. I hadn't used an alias when I joined. We had an ongoing arrangement to meet at the club. Which either of us could have put a stop to. We probably should have kept our interaction strictly to the club and not spent time together outside of it. We can chalk it up to an oversight.

"Now if it was to do with me coming to the compound, then you only had to let me know. I could have limited my time there or, at the very least, texted you when I was going to be around. Then maybe you wouldn't have felt the need to hide. I know how to be discreet. Good grief, what did you think I would do if I ran into you at Black Hawk? Say no introduction needed; he has been initiating me into the kinkier side of sex and fucking me senseless regularly," I stated, proud of myself for keeping my voice level and my focus on getting everything out and finished that I missed the expression change Max's face reflected. Instead, I continued because the quicker I finished, the quicker he would leave my house. "Honesty would have definitely helped the situation. You wouldn't have had to duck through doors, dart around corners, or hide in the shadows when I was around. I guess it was better late than never. From now on I'll be sure you're notified prior to me visiting the women or when I'll be swinging by to pick up Sawyer. Hopefully, that works for you. We are adults, after all. I think we can act accordingly, even though we will no longer be involved, it doesn't mean it has to be awkward when we cross paths at Black Hawk or at Whispering Nights. Though I want to ask you to please not treat Sawyer any different if you run into her at Ally's. She won't understand why if you treat her different and I would rather not have to answer her questions."

"Is that it? You finished?" Max asked in a deceptively low voice. The regret from earlier had gone from his eyes and replaced with anger. Since he was essentially getting what he wanted, I didn't entirely understand his anger. I made the break simple for him. My emotions were my problem. I would get over him, eventually.

"Yes. Though I was upset at the hospital, I appreciate you stopping by. We needed to clear things up. Now that we have, we can move on with no regrets." Intending to walk to the front door to let Max leave, I turned only to have Max grab my arm.

"Yeah, that shit isn't going to work for me."

"Why are you mad? I made it easy for you. You're getting what you want, Max." I jerked my arm out of his hand and glared at him.

"That's the problem. You don't have a fucking clue what I want!" Max said with his voice growing louder at the end.

"I don't know where you get off raising your voice at me. You aren't in charge here. This is my damn house, not the club where you're allowed to strut your dominant ass around and people have to listen. Leave before you wake Sawyer. It's getting late, and I really don't want to be up the rest of the night answering her questions."

"Shut up," he snapped.

"You don't tell me to shut up," I snarled. My blood pressure was rising if the heat I felt on my face was any sign.

"I did, so get over it. I listened to the bunch of shit you spewed, and now you are going to listen to me."

I opened my mouth to rip into him, but before I got a word out, he shook a finger in my face.

"Don't say a single word. If you do, I swear I will bend you over and spank your ass until you are screaming for me to fuck you. Fairly sure *that* will wake Sawyer, and you don't want to answer those questions. Do you?"

I glared at Max but closed my mouth. I was not only angry with him, but I was also angry with the response my

165

body had to his words. My stomach spasmed, my thighs tightened, and heat radiated in my core.

"For fuck's sake stop looking at me like that, or I won't get out what I need to say because I'll be taking care of the desire I see in your eyes. Damn it, I bet all I would have to do is strip you down, spread your legs wide, run my tongue through your pussy lips, and you would go off like a rocket." I blinked, shocked into silence, while Max groaned and closed his eyes. Running a hand across the back of his neck, he reopened his eyes and smirked. "Well, that sure didn't help. Christ, Gabriella, you drive me insane."

His expression caused me to laugh, which left me unable to keep the grin from forming. How was I expected to get over this man? The question had an instant sobering effect because I knew the answer—I wouldn't.

Chapter Seventeen

Flirt

Everything I ever wanted in an ol' lady stood in arm's reach and I was going to lose her. I wouldn't be able to live with myself if I did.

Gabriella had no clue how I felt about her outside of Whispering Nights, and the fault laid solely on my shoulders. I came to her house with the best of intentions and geared up to come clean when what happened? She started spitting out a ton of nonsense, which did nothing but make my blood pressure rise.

She doubted the time we had spent together as if it meant nothing to me. I made her doubt me. All because of my need to have her complete trust, though I hadn't extended the same courtesy to her. Staring at Gabriella, I knew I had to acknowledge my screwup to move forward. I couldn't afford not to. I refused to lose her over my stupidity.

"There are no excuses for what I did, but I'm going to try to explain, anyway." I took a deep breath, blew it out while I clenched and unclenched my hands. The need to pull her into my arms was pressing down on me. However, I knew if I touched her, the good intentions would be forgotten. I wanted more with Gabriella than just to dominate her sexually. I had tried to show her parts of me when instead of spending only time with her in the club, I had taken her out. I had wasted so much time with her because I couldn't bring myself to commit. She had been mine for months, and none of this would have happened if I had placed trust in her first.

"Are you planning to get on with it? It's been a long day and I'm tired and need to go to bed."

She would go to bed alright just not alone, and I had enough sense not to voice that out loud. Barely. The woman was determined to push all my buttons. Not that she didn't have a right to.

"You may not believe this, but I had planned to talk with you when we met this evening at Whispering Nights. I'll admit doing it in front of my brothers and ol' ladies at the hospital was not the best scenario. I could have stayed away until I knew you had left, but damn it, I wanted you to know. I needed it to get out so we could get past what I had done."

"Fine, we are past it. Is that all?"

None of this was going as I planned, I thought, then snorted when what my dad had said about vital information being left out of the planning popped in my head.

"Christ, the old man was right. I'm doing it again."

"Max, what are you talking about?"

"I'm dealing with a woman." Gabriella's facial expression changed. I physically saw her body stiffen. Her mouth opened, but before she could speak, I rushed on. "Being in control started long before I even knew what a dominant was. I was sure it had nothing to do with my mother leaving me with my dad after I was born. But

168

standing here facing everything I have ever wanted and feeling it slipping away has me torn. Torn because I should leave and give you time and space to digest everything, but... I can't. We can analyze my handling of it all later or not, because it doesn't change anything. To me control is like air and I need it as much to live. At least until you walked into Whispering Nights.

"I don't know how we didn't cross paths when Sawyer and Ally became friends and then you and the women by association. But I had no clue Brie and Gabriella were one and the same. When I met Sawyer for the first time was when I knew."

"Is that why you spent time with her? You figured out she was my daughter and thought you could get information about me out of her?"

"Maybe for like five seconds. She was shy one second, then the queen of questions. I hadn't paid much attention to kids until Ally came into the picture, then Neely. I never thought about having a family until my brothers started falling. Seeing them relaxed and happy was when I knew that was something I wanted. Being around Sawyer made everything clear to me. When Speed, Devil, and I were supposed to be teaching the girls self-defense and Sawyer dropped me to my knees, literally—that was it—she owned me. Nothing about my time spent around her had to do with you. You were already mine. Getting her in the deal is a bonus."

"What?"

"Christ, Gabriella, what did you think was happening when I suggested instead of going inside the club, we do something else?"

"That you were tiring of me and ready to move and having trouble telling me."

"Well, hell that was a direct hit to my ego. I thought if we did things that couples do together when they date, you might trust me enough and open up more about yourself. I have to say that you keep your personal stuff close to the vest. You'll be the perfect ol' lady."

"Excuse me?"

"Come on, Angel. Why would I dump you? Especially when I touch you like this." I reached out and, as gentle as I could, ran my hands down her arms. I clasped our hands together, then pulled her to me. I leaned forward and bent my face into her neck and placed a trail of kisses up her neck, then nipped her earlobe before sucking the sting away. "Or when I kissed you in the movie theater or while we were standing on the edge of the pier in the moonlight. Every single thing I did and do was to show you I wanted more. I wanted you. For fuck's sake, I need you," I whispered the last in her ear and received the first sign of hope when I felt a slight tremor from her body. I lifted my head intending to kiss her, but when I looked into her eyes, the sight of tears held me back.

"Aren't we the perfect pair? You have control issues, and I'm so out of touch with being a woman that I can't tell when a man is into me."

"Have you been listening? We are the perfect pair. I'll tell you what. I'll try to take it slow and work on toning down my control, which I make no promises. However, maybe I can up my dating skills, since they are evidently not strong enough for you to pick up on. Because no way you lack observation skills. During the process we can learn about each other. That will also give Sawyer a chance to get to know me in my new role as her mother's man."

"You're all she ever talks about when she comes home from visiting Ally. I think my daughter might be experiencing her first crush. My sister suggested that if you didn't respond when I told you I was falling for you, I should ask Sawyer to introduce me to Flirt. Evidently Sawyer spent a great deal of time talking to her aunt about you, too."

Gabriella didn't realize what she had let slip. She was falling for me and at some point had planned on telling me. My good intentions of going slow went out the window.

"Show me where your bedroom is, Angel."

Chapter Eighteen

Gabriella

"What?"

"Where is your bedroom, Gabriella?"

"Max, I don't think—"

"We have plenty of time to work on and cover what happened at the hospital. I know I was a dick. But damn it, you can't expect me to leave after hearing you say you're falling for me. I promise to let you tear into me for everything, but later."

"You deceived me for months and humiliated me in front of a room full of people. How do you expect me to just forget?"

"By letting me show you I'm sorry in the only way I know how. Later we can talk about anything you want. As far as forgiving me, I said before you can take your pound of flesh, and I'm positive the other women would willingly help you. You hold the power in this situation. If you ask me to go, I will. Just don't ask me to."

I had to be out of my mind for even considering letting Max take me to my bedroom, but I was, and the goosebumps that formed on my skin were definitely a sign that I not only enjoyed his possessive side—I enjoyed the softer side he had shown.

Max stood there and stared at me, saying nothing. Waiting for me to decide if he was going home or staying. My crushed feelings wanted me to walk to the door and hold it open for him to walk through while my eyes stared into his. He was right; I was falling. Truth be told, I was already there.

Wouldn't I have to be to have felt so betrayed and hurt?

My skin tingled with just a thought of what he would do to me. "Take me," came out as a whisper and I shiver from the change in his eyes. Could eyes hold so much desire?

"Get moving before I strip you here and fuck you on the couch. I would rather not take the chance Sawyer would walk in, but right now I'm not concerned enough to care. You're the only woman who has put my control to the test. The way I feel in this moment—the loss might burn us both up."

He barely touched my arm as we walked toward my room, but it was enough to have my center softening and nipples hardening. Once locked inside my bedroom, I thought he would be all over me and take me fast. Instead, he moved away from me and turned on the lamp on the nightstand.

"Strip and get onto the bed on your back with your neck resting on the edge of the mattress."

My stomach flipped, and my body shook in anticipation as I removed my clothes. Naked, I did as he instructed and laid on the bed. I watched upside down as he walked toward me, then stopped. I hadn't even noticed he'd removed his jacket and t-shirt.

What did that say about me?

I licked my lips when he undid his jeans and pushed them down to reveal he was commando and his cock was hard and ready. I watched as he moved his hand up and down his length. When the drop of pre-cum formed on the tip, I shivered.

"I love seeing the eagerness for my cock," he said as he stepped closer, then ran the head of his cock across my lips. The pre-cum moistening them. "Open wide, Angel. Suck my balls first, then after you have them dripping wet, I'll feed what you want most. If you are a good girl, I'll return the favor and eat you out."

I shifted and tilted my head back until I lined his balls up with my mouth. I licked, tongued, and sucked on them as he told me to. When he adjusted his stance, his balls were dripping, and he replaced them with his cock. Feeding it slowly.

"That's it. Take it all, Angel." I relaxed my throat and swallowed. The shaking of his thighs let me know he appreciated my effort.

The more I sucked him off, the more moisture I felt forming between my legs. I squeezed my thighs together to control the ache of wanting him inside me.

He demanded more, and I gave it to him. My reward was the touch of his hands coursing through my hair. His thumbs stroking my cheeks.

I swallowed as his cock touched the back of my throat and worked on breathing through my nose. His hands tightened in my hair as his warm release filled my mouth and his legs trembled.

He removed his cock and bent over, kissing me upside down, tasting himself on my lips and then my tongue as he devoured my mouth. When he broke the kiss, there were no soft words. He helped me up and turned me until my head was on the bed and my butt was on the edge.

"My turn," was the only warning I received before he dropped to his knees, lifted my legs until they rested on his shoulders and planted his face at my center.

The first swipe of his tongue had my eyes rolling back. The second had a moan escaping. When he sucked my swollen clit, my hips lifted. When he used the tip of his tongue to flick it and pushed a finger into my pussy, my head bent back and my back arched. As he feasted on me, I was on the verge of losing my mind. I came apart and exploded when I felt the pressure at my back hole.

"Scoot to the center and get up on your knees, Angel," Max said, then smacked my butt cheek, and I opened my eyes to find myself on my stomach with no memory of being flipped.

I crawled forward to make room for him, leaned on my arms, and rested my head on the bed. The bed dipped and then the warmth from Max's body surrounded me as he leaned over. One of his hands on the bed beside me and the other clasped at my hip.

I buried my face in the comforter and screamed when he entered me with one thrust. I had experienced Max's dominance at Whispering Nights, but this was different. This was ownership and he proved it as he rode me long and hard.

Chapter Nineteen

Flirt

"No way it's morning. Stop poking me and go back to sleep," I groused and rolled my shoulder to knock the finger that poked me away.

"It's morning and time for breakfast," the voice penetrated my ears, and my eyes shot open.

I looked over my shoulder into the face of a smirking Sawyer with messy bed hair as she stared at me from eyes like her mother's.

"Morning," I mumbled as I moved the hand on Gabriella's hip, shaking her.

"Are you eating breakfast with us?" Sawyer asked, then plopped down on the edge of the mattress behind me. I had never been more grateful for blankets. I was going to have to remember shorts the next time.

"Gabriella, Sawyer is up and wants breakfast," I said and shook her again.

"Why do you call my mom that? Everyone calls her Brie."

"Sawyer, halt the questions until after coffee, please," Gabriella said and lifted her head to see over my shoulder.

"'K, but is Flirt eating breakfast with us?"

I shifted my eyes to Gabriella, and she smiled. "Well, are you staying for breakfast?"

"If you're sure it's okay," I answered and lifted a brow.

"Yeah!" Sawyer yelled and moved off the bed. "I'll get all the stuff out," was said, then she darted out of the room.

Gabriella rested her head back on my arm, and her body started shaking.

"You find it funny your daughter busted me in your bed? Better yet, Sawyer hadn't looked shocked or traumatized about finding me here. How many men has she found in your bed?"

"No, what I find funny was the look on your face. You looked traumatized," Gabriella giggled. "And instead of being a grouchy ass with a side of rude in the morning, I would be more inclined to answer your other question. But not now." She shoved me to get up, and I tightened my grip.

"Not so fast. I'm sorry. I'm new to waking up with a kid poking me. Maybe I wouldn't have been so *traumatized* if I had some shorts on or at least underwear. Now answer my other question, and before you even think about not doing it or giving me some smartass response, I'll remind you we are still in the bedroom. The bedroom is the one place I have control, whether I have my dick inside you, or we are sleeping. Doesn't matter."

"You are the most aggravating man. You are the first man Sawyer has found in my bed. If you act naturally around kids, they won't think anything is wrong. Acting nuts draws their attention and kicks in their curiosity. We better get up since both of us are naked, and she will come back in if we don't show up in the kitchen soon. How did she even get into the room? You locked the door last night," Gabriella asked as we both got out of bed.

"I asked if you wanted it locked or unlocked before I turned the light out and got in bed. You said unlocked, so I unlocked it, then climbed into bed and pulled your already sleeping body into my arms," I told her as I pulled on my jeans and grabbed my t-shirt.

"The last thing I remember, and it is vague, is burying my face in the comforter so my scream was muffled and wouldn't wake Sawyer," Gabriella commented as she slipped into her sleep pants and a tank.

I smirked at her when my head popped through the neck of my t-shirt. "That's because I wore you out. I think you might have faded in and out of consciousness a couple of times toward the end."

"You know what? I'm not even going to argue about that because there is a strong possibility it is the truth."

I chuckled and draped my arm over her shoulder. "It is the truth. And it took a lot of energy to satisfy my woman, so what's for breakfast?"

"First coffee, then food."

"Sounds good and I'll sweeten the deal. You make coffee, and I'll throw breakfast together."

"You cook?"

"Yes, I do. I'm damn good at it. Though with it only being me, I don't do it much," I answered just as we reached the kitchen.

"Well, by all means, amaze me," Gabriella said, pinched my butt, and headed for the coffeepot.

"Can I help?" Sawyer asked.

"Sure thing. Let's get busy and show your mom what we can do."

Gabriella

Max, Sawyer and I spent most of the morning together, and it had been the best since Sawyer and I had moved to Shades Valley. It felt as if we were a family.

We ate breakfast, then while Sawyer and I cleaned up, Max ran home to shower and put on clean clothes.

When it came time for me to go to the hospital to circumcise Lock, Key, and Archer, I left Max and Sawyer on the couch watching cartoons.

Once I reached the hospital and had finished the circumcisions, I made my way to Luna and Sami's room. I wanted to let them know all went well and the babies would be brought back to them shortly. I'll admit my stomach felt as if it was filled with butterflies about facing the two women and possibly their men, too. So much had happened since I left their room yesterday.

When I reached the door to their room I hesitated, took a deep breath, then pushed the door open and walked in.

"Wondered if we'd see you today," Luna said no sooner than I entered.

Sami's eyes shot briefly to Luna, then they focused on me. "Did the boys do alright?" she asked while her eyes ran over me.

"Well, everything went as it was supposed to. They'll be brought to you in a bit. How are you both doing? Ready to get out of here and take your babies home?"

"God, yes," Luna expressed.

"Mac's releasing us in the morning," Sami supplied.

"Alright, the niceties are over, and we don't know how long it will be before someone stops by, so get on with what happened after you left yesterday," Luna demanded.

"Luna!" Sami snapped.

"What? You want to know as much as I do. You're just too sweet to come out and ask," Luna snapped back. When Sami stuck out her tongue, I chuckled. That was why I liked these women. They held nothing back—at least not in front of friends. I had learned that over the months of knowing them. It also caused a lump to form in my throat because they had accepted me into their fold and considered me a friend.

"You could have used a little more couth," Sami said and shook her head.

"Oh, please. That is a waste of energy. You can look at our friend and see Flirt wasted no time when he rushed out of here. The man took care of his business," Luna said, then turned her head toward me. "Are you going to deny it?"

I thought about lying just to ruffle Luna's feathers for a minute, but I couldn't do it. Especially knowing they felt horrible on my behalf yesterday. "I was crushed when I walked out. I felt humiliated..." I began and told them what happened from the time I left their room to Chad catching me as I was leaving the hospital. Max's dad, the drive home... everything. Letting it all out felt quite therapeutic. I purposely skipped the bedroom activity and jumped to the part where Sawyer found Max in my bed that morning. Once I caught them up, I added. "We still have things to work out, but we are invested in trying."

"Yeah, okay, that is all great. Super even. Awesome you forgave him. Since everything is out in the open, we want to know how dominant Flirt actually is?" Luna pointedly asked.

"Oh my God, I don't know who is nosier, you or Carly," Sami chided.

"Let's just say—controlling enough to make your toes curl, your skin heat, and your insides burn. And you will

181

gladly do anything he wants to experience those flames," I admitted.

Luna fanned herself. "Sweet Jesus, I'll never be able to look him in the eyes again."

"Look who in the eyes, baby?" Ghost asked as he walked in.

The three of us jerked our heads in his direction, and it surprised me cracking sounds weren't heard.

What I knew was I was not hanging around for Ghost to be answered.

"Well, got to run, ladies. Sawyer's probably wondering what's keeping me. See you later," I said and was out the door before anyone responded.

If any doubt remained in the recess of my mind that I'd let Max off too easily, they would have diminished the second I entered my house. The sound of Max's deep laughter and Sawyer's little girl giggles would have healed the deepest pain.

It was lunchtime when I got back home, and we opted to eat in town. We even enjoyed our food at the diner despite the attention we garnered.

After lunch, we hit the grocery store, then went back to my house and settled in. Max might have been surprised that morning with Sawyer. But as I watched them together, there was no way of missing the fact that my daughter indeed adored him, and if the way he talked to and carried on with her, the feeling was mutual.

By the time dinner was over and Max and Sawyer were on dish duty, I went to my room. After I pulled out the sealed envelope I had buried in a drawer, I slipped it into my purse. When the time came, I wanted to be prepared to share it with Max.

Chapter Twenty

Flirt

I opened the front door to my house and led Gabriella inside. Once we were in the living room, I reached up, grabbed ahold of her coat, and helped her out of it. For the first time I was nervous. I was ready for us to take the next step and holding back was something I wasn't used to.

"We're only here for the plates and cups. I didn't need to remove my jacket," she said and was frowning at me when she turned around.

I placed her jacket over the arm of the chair with mine and leaned in and kissed the crease between her brows the frown was making. "True, but I want to talk to you about something first, and I didn't want to wait until later, nor did I want an audience."

"Okay," she replied, still frowning at me.

"Stop, or you are going to have a permanent wrinkle," I said and lifted my hand and used a finger to smooth the spot between her brows that I just kissed.

I looked into her eyes and saw confusion and it irritated me for not planning better. Instead, when the realization hit after I watched her and Sawyer around the people who meant the most to me, I acted on impulse as the idea struck. The more I stood there and watched, the more I was against waiting. I wanted Gabrielle and Sawyer with me every day.

I dropped the hand I had lifted to her face only to grab both her hands with mine. "I want you and Sawyer to move in with me."

Gabriella stopped frowning, and I waited for her response. However, she said nothing. Instead, she pulled her hands from mine and turned toward the chair, lifting our jackets to reach her purse. She left the purse in the chair when we went to Speed's home. I watched as she opened it and reached inside. When she turned back to me, she held out a white envelope.

"What is this?" I asked as I accepted it, focused more on the envelope than the fact she hadn't responded to my question of them moving in.

"It's something I need you to read before I answer your question. You could change your mind," she said, and before I replied, she added. "Please," then walked to the couch and sat down.

"Alright." I joined her on the couch, flipped the unaddressed envelope and slid my finger under the flap. Once the seal was broken, I slid the folded paper out. After unfolding it, I silently read as Gabriella laid her head on my shoulder.

To the 2nd luckiest man,

*Before I get into the heart of the
letter, let me tell you why you are the*

second luckiest man. It's simple really. I was the first to experience life with Gabriella and to be loved by her.

I would hope you know the entire story by now. But I wouldn't be shocked if you don't because Gabs hasn't mentioned any of it to you. You will learn, if you haven't already, she keeps things close to her chest. Since you are reading this, the two of you have grown close enough that Gabs feels she's ready to take the next step with you.

Congrats. You will never meet a woman better than her. And you wouldn't have if I hadn't died. She was meant to be my future, but evidently, I wasn't meant to be hers. Cherish her and give her everything I had hoped to.

Anyway, back to the story. I was diagnosed with an inoperable brain tumor and given six months to live. It had come as a tremendous surprise. One I honestly could have done without.

A few days later after that terrific news, we found out Gabriella was pregnant. Instead of celebrating and moving our wedding date up, I had it canceled. I knew Gabs only went along because she thought I would change my mind after the shock of everything wore off. But my mind had never been clearer when I made the decision.

My refusal to discuss names for the upcoming baby whose life I would never be a part of—the child I would only be a name on a birth certificate or the man in pictures and stories others told him or her about—I just couldn't do that to him or her. Every child deserves a father in their life, not just the memory of one.

As you are reading this, you are probably thinking 'what an asshole'. Don't feel bad. Her family members have already labeled me as one. Hell, maybe I am. Does it really matter? I mean, considering as I write this, I'm almost out of time. It is what it is, and I have long since come to terms with it. If the decisions I have made are wrong, I will have an eternity to regret each of them.

Four months into my death sentence, I'm sitting in a chair composing this letter and watching Gabriella sleep. Today was long and hard with a single bright spot in the middle: the sonogram that revealed the baby we made is a girl—a daughter. The daughter I will never get to see, hold, or love—the one who will never know how my arms feel while wrapped around her as I hold her. She will never hear my whispered words as I rock her to sleep.

I'm hoping and praying that you have fallen in love with her as much as you have Gabs. I need you and she needs you to be the one to give her the comfort that only a dad can give.

As a dying man, I am going to believe you will and thank you. Thank you for accepting her as yours and taking on the role I couldn't fill for her. Also, I want you to share your name with her and make her part of your family by adopting her.

I'm also going to thank you for all the times you will pick her up when she falls.

Hold on to her as she cries.

Slay every monster for her.

Give advice to her that only a father can.

Protecting her until the day comes when another man vows to take the job over for you. And even then, as you step back and place her hand in his, it will be as her dad because you will hold the knowledge that you will always be the first man she fell in love with. A gift I wish would have extended to me.

Mostly, though, thank you for loving her and Gabs enough. I know if she is anything like her mother, you will be blessed beyond what you could imagine.

I don't feel the need to tell you what a remarkable woman Gabriella is. You have gotten this far, so you must know.

I will end this by asking you to take care of them. I assure you being with Gabs will make you a better man—it did me.

Justin Sawyer
Luckiest Man #1

I folded the letter and slipped it back into the envelope and set it on the side table, then I put an arm around Gabriella's shoulder and pulled her closer to me. With her head now resting against my chest, she wiped at the tears running down her cheeks. Neither of us spoke. We sat quietly, each of us absorbed with our own thoughts.

For me, Justin's words only solidified everything I already knew. If Gabriella and I were lucky enough to have more children, Sawyer would never have a reason to feel as if she didn't belong or wasn't truly part of my family. She would be my daughter, would always hold a special place in my heart. She belonged to me as if I had taken part in her creation. She was as much mine as the woman who sat beside me and the man who wrote a letter wanting me to assume the role he never got to fulfill.

At that moment if I had talked to Justin, I would have told him he hadn't needed to tell me what being with Gabriella would do to me. I was already on the road to being a better man because she had walked into my life when I least expected and had needed her the most.

I touched my lips to the top of Gabriella's head, then turned my head and rested my cheek against the spot I had kissed.

"Well, I guess I'm going to have to do better than asking you to move in here with Sawyer," I said and had to lift my head when Gabriella lifted hers so she could look up at me.

"What are you talking about?" she asked, and I leaned down and planted a kiss on the wrinkled spot between her brows caused again by her frowning.

"Well, I'm thinking the woman who is going to make a home with me should, at the very least, have the same last name as my daughter and I. In fact, I'm going to insist on it."

She stared at me and blinked a few times before her expression changed, and her dark eyes showed a glimmer of humor. "Hmm… you realize in this day and time lots of women marry but keep their maiden names instead of taking their husband's. And some never marry, they just live together."

"You are right. However, none of those women are mine. You are, so you will have the same last name."

"Wow, that has to be the most romantic proposal any woman has ever received. I should write it down for future generations to study and learn from." Gabriella laughed, and I adjusted, then stood with her in my arms.

"I can be romantic," I remarked and headed toward the stairs. "If I try," I added as I climbed them.

"Oh my goodness, be still my heart," she said, and with her free hand, the one not wrapped around my neck to hold on, she patted her heart for effect.

"Smartasses get spanked, but I'll keep count and give you your punishment another time." I walked into my bedroom and kicked the door closed. Holding on to her with one arm while I used the hand on my other arm to throw the lock—just in case anyone stopped by to see what was keeping us. What I should have done was flip the lock on the front door when we passed, but my head had been preoccupied.

"Punishment?" she asked. The previous humor in her voice was gone.

"Yes. All bad girls receive punishment." If I weren't concentrating on keeping my desire tamped down, I would have laughed at the wide-eyed look Gabriella was giving me.

"You will not spank me. I wasn't even spanked as a child," she said as I shifted her in my arms until we were chest to chest, then I slowly let her body slide down mine. When her feet hit the floor, I moved my hands into the hair on the sides of her head and held her in place as I looked down at her.

"You have enjoyed everything I've done so far. Trust me when I say you will enjoy the punishment part, too."

"No, I won't. Why do you think it was on my list? No pain period. Spanking involves pain."

"Angel, we will work on your ideas of what is painful, but later. We have a lifetime ahead of us to break you in properly. Right now, I'm going to show you I can be gentle if I work at it." I leaned down and kissed her, putting a stop to anything she would have said. Her lips were soft, warm, and inviting, as always. I sucked her bottom lip between mine and bit down gently, then touched my tongue to the spot before running it over the seam. Gabriella opened her mouth, and I pushed my tongue in. Our tastes combined while I explored every crevice.

She placed her hands at my waist and melted into me. The kiss went on until I broke it to bury my face between her neck and shoulder to gain my breath. I was acutely aware of her breasts rising and falling as she fought her own battle to get her breathing under control.

"I do trust you. You are gentle, Max. I have seen it with Sawyer and your brothers' kids. I think you have a habit of putting everyone's needs before your own. It's like second nature to you. It has nothing to do with you having to be in control of everything, either. It's because you are a caring and loving man."

There were no words for how Gabriella made me feel. Instead, I was determined to show her what she brought out in me that no other woman had. I ran my hands down her arms until I reached her wrists. After wrapping my fingers around them, I pulled, and she released her hands at my waist. I took a step back and let go of her wrists only to reach for the hem of her shirt. My fingers clasped the material and in one swift move, I had the shirt off, then it was flittering to the floor. I dropped to my knees and reached first for her right foot and removed her shoe and sock. After doing the same to her left foot, I reached for the front of her jeans, unfastening them and working them down her legs until she lifted each foot up, freeing her from the pants. I stood with her in front of me in nothing but a black lace thong and matching bra.

Reaching out and taking hold of her shoulders, I turned her and made fast work of removing her bra. With a finger curled on each side of the tiny band on the thong, they soon followed the rest of her clothes, topping off the pile already on the floor. Everything about Gabriella called to me: her scent, her taste, her touch.

Everything with her overloaded my senses. Before I knew it, I was trailing kisses and taking nips as I worked my way down her neck, then across her collarbone, and down until I reached her breasts. Tonguing one nipple, then biting gently only to move my mouth over and do the same to the other breast. I pinched each peaked nipple between two fingers and worked them until Gabriella moaned and clasped her hands on my shoulders, digging her nails into my skin.

My cock throbbed behind the material of my jeans, impatient and anticipating the feel of her warm, wet heat wrapped around me. I wanted to spread her wide and take her hard and fast, but I refused to rush. Gabriella deserved so much more, and I would at least give her everything I had in me.

I snatched the covers on the bed and yanked them down, then swooped her up into my arms. I placed a knee on the bed and laid her down in the middle. After I discarded my clothes, I joined her.

Kissing her to rekindle the flames, I then started my journey down from her lips to her neck as if following a trail. I stopped to give her breasts attention on my way down. Next, a brief stop at her stomach as I circled my tongue around her belly button. Each hipbone received a kiss. All the while, my hands followed.

By the time I reached my destination, her hands were in my hair, tugging as if to guide me where she needed me the most.

I slid my hands down her body until I reached her thighs, and then I spread her wide. With no hesitation, I stuck my tongue out and licked her from back to front, tasting her, enjoying every moan she released from my efforts. My own groans mixed with hers were the only sounds in the room. As I pushed my tongue through her folds, her back arched, and she dug her nails into my scalp.

"Max," came out of her mouth on a scream when I sucked her clit between my lips. Then I circled the nub with the tip of my tongue and pushed a finger into her and felt her thighs tremble against my head. "More! Oh my God, I need more!"

Adding a finger into her depths, I pushed in and out as I bit down on the nub that was swelling and peeking out from its hood, plump and pink. Flattening my tongue, I put pressure on her clit while I shoved my fingers in as deep as they would go, then pulled my tongue away and sucked the bundle of nerves into my mouth. Her orgasm hit fast, and I deftly used my fingers to help her ride out the tremors.

Once her body went lax, I worked my way back up her body until I laid between her legs, hot, hard, and aching for my release. Holding my weight on one arm, I leaned down until our lips met. She opened, and I slid my tongue in, sharing her taste with her.

Leaning to the side, I reached down with my free hand and grasped my cock, running the head through her folds. Heat radiated from her center, and I could not hold off any longer. I placed my cock at her entrance, then moved my hand, grabbed behind her knee, and shoved her leg up and out until she was spread wide for me.

With a single snap of my hips, I filled her. I gritted my teeth and held still to give Gabriella a few seconds to adjust. When she shifted her hips, I groaned.

"I need you to move, Max. Please." The last word came out breathlessly as she wiggled under me.

I eased out, then eased back in. Keeping the pace slow and steady as I leaned down and used my mouth and teeth on her nipples while quashing the need to let go of the orgasm that had been building since my first lick of her.

"Please, faster, harder, I need to come, Sir," Gabriella said as she moved her head from side to side on the mattress. Her hips rising and falling. Her hands grasping the covers at her sides.

I knew she was unaware of what she said. She only referred to me that way when we were at the club. It wasn't something I required outside of play. But coming from her, and in the middle of my struggle to keep up the gentle pace, I lost it—my hard-earned control broken by the woman under me.

Raising up, I let go of her leg, pulled out, grabbed her hips, and flipped her over. I lifted her until she was on her knees, my body in position behind her. I used one hand to gather her thick hair, and holding on to it while my other hand held her hip, I thrusted into her and moved in earnest, pounding into her as I held her head up with her hair.

All the way out, then back in. Bottoming out each time. The pace fast and hard. Skin slapping on skin mixed with the sounds of heavy breathing, groans, and grunts. The headboard hitting intermittently against the wall.

Instead of the familiar sign of tightness building in my gut. I felt as if a stream of fire ran through my body and down my spine until it pierced its way to my balls. They drew up, and I knew the end was imminent. I slammed in one last time, held in place as Gabriella spasmed around me, milking every drop from me until my knees weakened and shook.

After I pulled out, released the grip I had on her hair and hip, she plopped down on the bed. I followed barely able to shift enough to land on my back beside her instead of on top of her.

I closed my eyes and worked to steady my breathing. The air from the fan above the bed cooling my damp, overheated skin. Not sure how much time went by before I opened my eyes and lifted my arm as Gabriella rolled on her side and fitted into the spot I made, resting her head on my chest. I draped my arm down behind her and made lazy circles on her back with my fingertips.

"That was pretty damn hot romancing, mister," she said.

I would have laughed if I had had an ounce of energy left, but I found enough to speak. "I lost it toward the end."

"Yes, and it was wonderful. It ended with a bang. I certainly couldn't have asked for more," she said, then swatted at my hand when I chuckled and pinched her ass.

"I guess the only thing left is to say 'yes,'" she said and bent her head back and smiled up at me.

Angling my head and shifting my eyes to the side to see her better, I asked, "Yes, to what?"

"For pete's sake, I can't believe you. Yes, to marrying you," she said. Her smile gone, replaced with a glare.

It took everything in me not to laugh. "Funny, I don't remember asking that question," I answered, then flinched when she twisted my nipple. Grabbing her hand from ripping it off, I pushed up from the bed, shifted Gabriella in my arms, and headed toward the bathroom so we could shower.

"What are you doing?"

"We need to shower," I said as I set her on her feet and opened the shower door, then turned the water on.

"We don't have time to shower. We were only supposed to get the plates and cups. Everyone is going to be wondering what has taken so long. I cannot face them. They are going to know what we were doing." I wrapped my arms around her and kissed her to stop her panicked rambling. When I pulled away from the kiss, I turned her and led her into the shower stall.

"If we don't shower, they will know for sure when we walk in the door smelling like sex." When she hit my shoulder, I chuckled.

"I'm glad you think it is funny. I will never be able to look any of them in the eyes again," she said and reached up, grabbing her hair and doing some twisting until it was bunched up at the back of her head.

I moved to where my body blocked most of the spray, so her hair would only be dampened while she washed off, instead of soaked. "Have you noticed all the kids running around? My brothers know about sex and have had it frequently. I mean, you went to medical school and you are a kid's doctor. You know how they are made," I teased as I washed my body.

195

"Aren't you just the funniest man," she said, bending over to wash her legs. When she stood back up, she froze and stared at me.

"Angel, it will be okay. No one will say a word. Except maybe Carly... or Luna."

"I'm not thinking of them. I was thinking about the fact we didn't use a condom... again. I not putting the blame on you, I'm responsible, too. It's that we have been really lax using them other than at the club," she answered.

"It will be alright."

"Max, I'm on the pill, but it isn't a hundred percent. Sawyer is proof of that."

"Alright, then stop taking the pill," I said and stuck my head under the spray to rinse my hair.

"Hello, that's definitely a surefire way to become pregnant!" she said, her voice rising at the end.

"Usually is. I was hoping since I'm already getting a daughter, you might give me a son next time around. The odds are in our favor, since boys seem to be popping out everywhere lately." In the last month, Jag's and Devil's sons were born two weeks apart. The boys officially had the girls seven to three, four with Sawyer added to the mix.

Gabriella looked at me and her eyes softened. "Are you sure about all this, Max? I don't want you to feel pressured into becoming Sawyer's dad because of Justin's letter. With you asking us to move in, I felt you needed to read it. I have been carrying it around for a while now. If you adopt and they add your name to her birth certificate, she will legally be yours. I know I shouldn't have gone along with Justin's wishes. I honestly think he thought or, better yet, wanted me to find someone to replace him before I had the baby. He would mention daily how he didn't want me to spend months grieving for him. He might have lived five months after his diagnosis, but honestly, I lost him the same day he found out. When he handed me that letter and said to put it away until I met the man I knew I wanted a future with, I literally wanted to scream at him. Then he let me read it before he sealed the envelope. I was so damn mad I wanted to rip it up, but the look on his face stopped me. He said it was the one thing he could do for his daughter, and I just couldn't take that from him," Gabriella said as we finished and stepped out of the shower.

"First, Justin was dying, and he knew nothing was going to change that. He was probably trying to deal with everything the best he could under the circumstances. Did he make a few poor decisions along the way? Maybe to others, but he felt he was doing the best for you and his unborn daughter. I can't even imagine what it took for him to make those decisions. I wouldn't have acted so selflessly. I would have married you as soon as we left the doctor's office so there would always have been a legal document showing you were once mine. Even if it wasn't for forever. I would have wanted to be listed as the father on my daughter's birth certificate, whether later you found someone else and let him adopt her or not. She would have taken her first breath belonging to me. So, I might disagree with the way Justin handled everything, but Sawyer is mine. The paperwork is just so others will know it, too. I love you both, Gabriella. It's as if I was only marking time in my life waiting for the two of you to show up."

With tears running down her cheeks, Gabriella grabbed hold of my arms and went up onto her toes to reach my mouth. She kissed my lips, then pulled back and smiled. "We are the lucky ones. I love you, Max, and I know Sawyer does, too. I love you even when you're bossy and arrogant."

"Hmm… I'll claim bossy, but arrogant I am not. I just state facts," I answered haughtily, and it had the effect I wanted it to on Gabriella. She burst out laughing, and I grinned unable to hold on to the stern look I projected.

We toweled off, then dressed. Gabriella only had to use the blow dryer for five minutes since her hair hadn't gotten too wet. Once we were ready, we went downstairs and put our jackets back on. I jogged to the kitchen and grabbed the package of plates and the package of cups I kept in the pantry, then we headed out of the house. As we walked back to Speed and Sami's place, we discussed everything we needed to do to get Gabriella and Sawyer moved in, to when we would marry.

"Do you have a favorite diamond cut?"

"Not at all. Surprise me. I'm sure I will love whatever you pick out."

"Yeah, you can come to the jewelry store with me and pick it out. No way am I falling into that trap," I said and chuckled when she elbowed me.

While we had been walking back to Speed's, something kept niggling in the back of my mind. As we reached the front door, I opened it and let Gabriella walk in ahead of me. From the sounds that greeted us, coming from two directions, a group was in the living room, and a group was in the kitchen. I closed the door behind us and hadn't taken another step when it hit me.

"You named her after him," I said and shook my head that it hadn't registered before then.

Gabriella looked up at me and smiled. "Yes, Sawyer Justine. It was the only way to give her a part of him."

I leaned in and placed my lips against her smiling ones and gave her a brief kiss. "Angel, you are a beautiful woman, both inside and outside."

"I thought I heard the front door. It's hard to tell with so much noise," Speed said as he walked out of the opening from the living room into the hallway.

"We're back with the plates and cups. Are the women in the kitchen? I will take them in there," Gabriella said, a blush forming on her cheeks as she grabbed the packages out of my hands and rushed off toward the kitchen at the other end of the hallway.

Speed chuckled, then slapped me on the shoulder before we walked into the living room. Sawyer sat on the floor with Ally, Neely, and Paxton, playing a board game. Coast was sitting by Tracker on the floor with game controllers in their hands and gunfire coming from the speakers on the big screen TV in front of them. Crusher sat in one chair holding Archer, Speed's son, while Devil sat in the other chair holding his two-week-old newborn, Brock. Jag was on one end of the sectional, bouncing Poppy on one knee while holding his less than a month-old sleeping son, Gabe, in one arm. Ghost was on the opposite end of the sectional with his twins, Lock and Key, one in each arm, laying against his chest. At his feet, Karma their rescued German Shepherd, laid keeping watch.

"Any more kids and we're going to have to use the clubhouse when everyone gets together," I said to Speed, drawing my other brothers' attention.

"That or we are going to have to build on to our places," Crusher answered.

"Hey, about time you made it back. We thought we were going to have to form a search party," Ghost said, and the others chuckled. The only thing that kept them from making any other remarks was the kids in the room.

Sawyer finally looked up from the game she was playing. "Where's my mom?"

"She's in the kitchen," I answered.

"What took you so long to come back?" she asked.

"Yeah, brother. What took you so long?" Devil repeated, his lips twitching to keep from laughing while the others all wore smirks and waited to see how I was going to answer.

I knew exactly what to say to wipe those smirks off their faces. I looked at Sawyer when I answered, "Well, I wanted to get your mom alone so I could ask her to marry me." No one in the room needed to know the original plan was to ask her to move in. They only needed to know the end result.

Smirks gone and replaced with dropped jaws, then followed by huge grins once the initial shock was over, made me wish I had had my phone out when I announced it. I could have taken a picture of my brothers' faces to show them every time they got on my nerves.

Sawyer wasn't wearing a look of shock when she stood and ran toward me. As she jumped, I caught her in my arms. "Are you really marrying my mom? Are we going to live with you? Can the bedroom in the front be mine so I can look out the window and see Ally's house? Am I going to get a brother or sister? Will you be like my dad?"

"Hold up. Are you going to give me a chance to answer any of your questions?" I asked, hoping to stop the barrage of hers. It worked, and she nodded and stared at me out of her deep brown eyes. I was going to be running off boys left and right as she got older.

Sawyer nodded.

"Okay, here goes. Yes, I am going to marry your mom. Yes, you will live with me. Yes, you can have the front bedroom. I hope one day you will have a brother or a sister. Maybe both. And to answer your last question—I won't be *like* your dad." Sawyer's face fell, and I squeezed her, then finished. "I will *be* your dad. You were always meant to be mine. It just took a little time for us to find each other." I hugged her tighter when she buried her face in my neck and cried.

"Well, shit, if you are finished bomb dropping, let's celebrate," Jag said, then he looked at Ally, who was staring back at him. "I'll pay you as soon as my hands are free and I can reach my wallet."

I chuckled, then glanced to the doorway that led into the kitchen and saw Gabriella standing there, her hands fisted at her mouth while the other women stood behind her. Every one of them wiping their eyes.

Chapter Twenty-One

Gabriella

I felt my face flaming as I rushed down the hallway toward the kitchen. I wasn't sure what to expect from the women, but I knew I could handle their ribbing better than the men's.

When I walked into the kitchen, the women were talking to each other as they each worked on different tasks to get dinner set up buffet style on the island.

"Where do you want these?" I asked, holding up the paper plates and plastic cups as all heads whipped in my direction.

"Look who finally made it back. Did you and Flirt have to make the plates and cups? We thought we were going to have to eat without you guys," Carly said, then snickered. The other women shook their heads and rolled their eyes while my face felt as if it was going to burst into flames.

"Ignore her, Brie. You can put a stack there," Sami said as she pointed to the open space at one end of the bar, "then place the rest inside the pantry to get the packages out of the way. Flirt can take those back to his place when you guys are ready to leave. It's probably what he regularly eats on so he doesn't have to wash dishes."

"Dominic would use them at every meal. He cooked dinner last week when I had a meeting after school, and I came home to a spaghetti-soaked paper plate in the microwave," River said.

"We don't even have paper plates in the house. Emery does most of the cooking, and I've never seen him use one, even for a sandwich," Mac said as she looked over her shoulder at us while putting together a salad.

"We don't use them either, but I admit, it would come in handy. I do all the cooking now since I came home to Lance's idea of a hearty dinner of beans and weenies. Thank goodness I prepared meals ahead of time before Brock was born because I don't think I could have handled any of Lance's cooking," Bailey said, and I grinned when I saw her glance at the doorway that led into the living room. I could hear the noise from the TV and the men talking, but I couldn't make out what they were saying.

Surprised Sawyer hadn't come to look for me, I leaned as far as I could over the island to look into the living room. I could see Coast on the floor with Tracker, and Sawyer and the other kids sitting on the floor playing a game around the coffee table, but for the other men and babies, they were out of view from my position.

"Please, what do you think Brax and I have been eating on since we brought the boys home? Washing dishes is one less chore to do," Luna said, then reached over and snatched a cucumber slice from the cutting board Mac was using and popped it into her mouth.

"Bitch, like you do that many fucking chores by yourself. I know for a damn fact Shakes helps you out, and

204

Ghost hardly lets you lift a finger when he is home," Carly said, and I smiled when Luna flipped her off.

It hadn't taken me long after meeting all the women to realize that Sami, Bailey, River, and Mac were calm compared to Carly and Luna. They were fun to be around, and they had welcomed Sawyer and me into the fold before Max had even come into the picture.

When I first moved to Shades Valley and started my practice, I questioned daily my decision to move Sawyer and me away from our family. Since meeting the women and men of Black Hawk, it was feeling more like home.

"Shakes comes over and watches the boys so I can shower and get a few things done. It isn't as if she's doing chores and waiting on me while I sit on my butt. And the motivation behind Brax helping is because he hopes I will give him at least one more kid. The man has it in his head that we need a little girl to round out our family. I told him we could revisit that idea later after I've had time to forget what childbirth felt like. Besides, if the boys don't slow down on my nipples, I will need to have reconstructive surgery. The way the two go at them, they are definitely going to be breast men," Luna said and rolled her eyes.

All of us smiled, but then started laughing when Sami, River, Bailey, and I replied "I have a daughter he can have."

"Yeah, thanks, but no thanks. Ally has no filter. Neely has a temper. Sawyer doesn't talk; she questions. Poppy... well, okay, maybe Poppy. She's still young enough and hasn't picked up any bad habits from you and Jag," Luna said, looking over at River.

"Pfft, our girls," River said, pointing to Sami, Bailey, me, then to her own chest, "on their worst day will never be as bad as a little girl you have."

"I am so hurt," Luna said, placed her hand over her heart, and batted her eyelashes. I laughed, enjoying the women's antics and the fact their focus wasn't on me. I wanted to share about marrying Max with my friends, but I thought Sawyer needed to be told first.

"We all might believe that if you had fucking feelings to hurt," Carly replied as she pulled the aluminum foil off a huge pan of chicken. Then set it on the island with the various other steaming bowls of food.

"I was going to be the bigger person, but with that remark, I hope you have cash on hand," Luna said, and the smile she gave Carly made her look sinister.

"For what?" Carly sneered.

"To pay Ally for cursing when I tell her," Luna said, then laughed at Carly's expression.

"You are a mean and evil woman," Carly replied and pursed her lips. "Hey, wait a minute. We only pay her if she is around to hear, so it doesn't matter if you tell. I don't have to fork over cash to her."

"I'm surprised she didn't hear you and run in here. Yesterday while she and Neely were at the house playing video games with Paxton, and I was paying bills online at the kitchen table, my elbow hit my glass knocking it over. I said 'fucking hell,' and before I could get up to grab a dishtowel, Ally walks in with her hand out and says she heard me. Evidently, she was coming out of the hall bathroom. The girl has the hearing of a bat," Mac said, then turned to the stove when the timer buzzed and picked up the potholder off the counter.

"Is there anything else that needs to be done?" I asked, looking around the kitchen.

"With the rolls Mac is pulling out of the oven, dinner is ready," Bailey said.

"I feel bad you guys had to do all the cooking," I apologized, then moved around the island toward the living room doorway. "I will tell everyone dinner's ready."

Just as I reached the doorway, I opened my mouth to inform everyone about dinner, but froze instead when I heard Sawyer's voice, "Are you really marrying my mom? Are we going to live with you? Can the bedroom in the front be mine so I can look out the window and see Ally's house? Am I going to get a brother or sister? Will you be like my dad?"

I stood unmoving and stared at Max with Sawyer in his arms. My daughter's eyes shined with happiness.

"More than mattress bouncing happened at Flirt's," came from Carly and I knew the women had heard. I felt their presence behind, but never took my eyes off Sawyer and Max.

"Hold up. Are you going to give me a chance to answer any of your questions?" Max asked, and I watched as she stared at Max and nodded. "Okay so here goes. Yes, I am marrying your mom. Yes, you will live with me. Yes, you can have the front bedroom. I hope one day you will have a brother or a sister. Maybe both. And to answer your last question—I won't be *like* your dad." At Max's last answer, I watched Sawyer's happy expression turn to one of hurt. Before I could even process why he would say that to my daughter, he continued. "I will *be* your dad. You were always meant to be mine. It just took a little time for us to find each other." Sawyer buried her face in his neck, and I knew from the shaking of her body that she was crying.

Who wasn't? I thought when I heard sniffling behind me and felt tears on my cheeks.

I knew one of the men said something to Ally, but my focus stayed on Max. He glanced toward the doorway and our eyes met. I hadn't even remembered walking toward the two until Max held out one of his arms and I moved in and wrapped my arms around them both. We stayed wrapped up in our own little world until someone said, "Let's eat before the food gets cold?"

"Can we move after dinner?" Sawyer asked when she raised her head off Max's shoulder. I moved to his side, shook my head, and smiled when she lifted the bottom of her shirt to wipe her red-rimmed eyes.

I wasn't sure how to answer her, but before I could, Max did, "After dinner, we'll pick up some stuff for you and your mom and any other important things you need to stay at the house. Next weekend, we'll start moving the rest. There's a bed already in the front bedroom, and you can sleep on that until we move your bedroom furniture in. Does that work for you, ladies?"

"Works for me," Sawyer said and smiled as Max put her down.

"Glad that's settled. Let's go into the kitchen before the food disappears. Since running over to the house and back, I am suddenly starving," Max said, and I pinched his waist where my hand rested. He chuckled and started leading us toward the kitchen, and when Sawyer grabbed his hand, it took everything in me not to cry again.

"Can I call you dad now, or do I have to wait until you and mom get married?" Sawyer asked, and at Max's abrupt stop, it had Sawyer and me stopping alongside him.

"Do you want to?" Max answered hoarsely, then looked at me, and I smiled to convey it was okay with me if he was okay with it.

"Yep. I got pictures of my dad that Mom showed me, but he died before she had me. I don't have anyone to call dad like the other kids do," Sawyer said, shrugging her shoulders while she looked up at Max.

"You know what?"

"What?" Sawyer asked.

"I've never had anyone call me dad, so I think it's an excellent idea. Don't you?" Max said.

I picked up on the strain in his voice, but Sawyer hadn't. A grin split her face and had me wiping at the lone tear that escaped.

"Uh huh, cause I've been waiting for you, too… Dad," Sawyer said, then pulled her hand from Max's and headed toward the kitchen, not realizing when she used the words he said earlier, it had nearly undone him.

I squeezed his waist, then moved my hand to his and rubbed circles while I asked, "You going to be okay?" I realized listening to Sawyer, that Justin may have been right about her having more than memories of a dad. She needed one in her everyday life.

Max took a deep breath and blew it out, then ran a hand down his face before he looked at me. "Yes, I am. I think I am going to be more than just okay," he said and smiled. We had walked again when he gave an unhumorous chuckle. "Fuck, I owe a debt to Justin, and there is no way I'll ever be able to pay it. He died, and I gained everything I wanted. He at least deserves a visit to his gravesite when we go to Las Vegas so I can meet your family."

No decision I would make about my life from that moment on would top the one to move to Shades Valley. If I hadn't made a move, I would never have met Max, and what an unfathomable thought that was.

"We'll have to make plans to do that," I said as we entered the crowded kitchen and moved to where Sawyer stood with the other kids so I could help fill her plate.

"We've got plenty of time. Right now you need to eat, Angel," Max said, and I felt him kiss the back of my head as he leaned around me and grabbed a plate. "I'll fix yours why you help Sawyer."

"And there, brothers, is the sound of the last man falling," Crusher said, and the other men, who stood on the other side of the island beside him, laughed. Then the typical ball and chain jokes started.

"It takes a while, but they grow on you," Bailey said beside me as she helped Neely.

"How? Like a fungus," I joked as I placed a roll on Sawyer's plate. The room went quiet for long enough that I worried I might have misspoken until everyone burst out laughing—even the kids, whether or not they understood.

Max ran his hand from the top of my head down the back of my hair, then he said, "Welcome to the family, Angel."

Chapter Twenty-Two

Flirt

After grabbing a beer and pouring Gabriella a glass of wine, I went into the living room. I set her glass on the coffee table and my beer on the side table before I took a seat on the couch. Hearing the timbre of voices making their way downstairs, I smiled, leaning my head back until it rested against the couch. I closed my eyes at the calming effect of Gabriella's laughter and Sawyer's giggles ran over me.

I ran my work schedule through my head and made a mental list of everything that needed to be done, scheduled, or taken care of to make this home as much Gabriella's and Sawyer's as it was mine.

After we had finished dinner and polished off dessert, which consisted of Claire's, Bailey's mom, and my dad's woman, bakery confections. The three cupcakes I had stuffed in my mouth had only added to my overstuffed feeling from dinner. I knew if I had kicked back and relaxed for even fifteen minutes after eating, I wouldn't have wanted to move. So, I went to my house, grabbed Gabriella's purse, got in my truck and drove to the garage behind Speed's. After I tossed a few empty shipping boxes from parts deliveries into the back of the truck, I drove to the front of the house and picked up Gabriella and Sawyer.

The trip to town to pack up some things they would need over the next week took two hours. Then another two hours helping my girls get situated once we were back at the house.

Footsteps had my eyes opening, and my thoughts bouncing back to the present. I turned my head to the side and watched as Sawyer padded barefoot into the living room, wearing her pajamas and holding Gabriella's hand.

"Will you tuck me in?" she asked before she made it across the living room.

"Max is tired, baby girl. Tell him goodnight, and I'll tuck you in," Gabriella told her.

"How about your mom and I both tuck you in," I said and stood. No way would I miss her first official tuck in at my house, no matter how tired I was.

"Okay," she answered with an exuberance only a kid could have after a long day.

When I reached them, I swooped Sawyer up, forcing her to drop Gabriella's hand, and swung her around until she sat on my shoulders. The sound of her and Gabriella laughing had me smiling.

I walked up the stairs with Gabriella following behind. When we reached the bedroom that faced the front of the house, I walked to the bed and unceremoniously flipped Sawyer off my shoulders and onto the bed. After her body bounced a few times, making her giggle, she climbed under the covers and laid her head on the pillow.

Once Gabriella had given Sawyer a kiss and told her goodnight, she stepped back, and I took her place. I bent and kissed Sawyer's forehead. "See you in the morning."

"'Kay," she answered and closed her eyes.

When we got back downstairs to the living room, I plopped down on the couch. "She was out fast."

Gabriella grabbed the glass of wine I had set on the table, then sat down beside me. She curled her legs to the side and leaned her head on my shoulder. "She had an exciting day. We all have."

"In the best of ways," I said, and lifted my arm and placed it around Gabriella's shoulders.

"Oh, yes. As a matter of fact, you're not the only one who owes Justin. I think I do, too. If he hadn't talked about the short time he lived here, I wouldn't have brought Sawyer to see where her dad had grown up. Heck, I had never heard of Shades Valley before Justin spoke of it," Gabriella said absently and took a sip of her wine.

My brows furrowed, and I asked, "Justin spent time in Shades Valley?"

She leaned forward to set her glass on the table, then snuggled back into me before she answered sleepily, "Uh huh."

"Fuck me, the name hadn't even registered when I read the letter. When you mentioned him before, you referred to him only by his first name. Hell, my brothers and I went to high school with a Justin Sawyer."

"Max, what are you talking about?" She lifted her head and looked at me, confusion showing in her eyes.

"The Justin Sawyer I knew transferred into Shades Valley High as a Junior. We were in the same homeroom along with Coast and Devil. He was our friend, and he hung around with us all the time. Hell, we taught him how to ride a motorcycle. Back then Dare had an old bike that finally gave out and he bought a new one. Instead of junking it, the others and I asked if we could have it to work on. The first bike we ever rebuilt. Justin worked part-time after school

213

because all he ever talked about was aging out and hitting the road. We'd told him he would need a ride, and since we all had bikes, he could have the one we were working on. He bought the parts and helped us work on the bike. Took us over two months to get that bike done. My dad took him to get his license. I had never seen him smile as much as he did when he held the license in his hand.

"He was smart and easy-going unless you pissed him off. Sometimes we would forget he had been in the system since his parents died in a car accident that he had survived. The authorities hadn't been able to find any relatives, so he went into the system at five years old.

"The Swanson's house was his tenth foster family. They hated when he started hanging around with us. He didn't give a shit what they thought, though. By the time he came to them, he knew more about the system than they did. The system turns out three types of kids; shy and withdrawn or hardened by life. The third is the small percent, the ones who refuse to let the system break them and go against some hefty odds to succeed.

"Every time we would go by the Swanson's house, they would threaten him with being pulled, and remind him the next stop would be a group home. The threat only showed how much they didn't know or even try to get to know Justin. By the time graduation rolled around each of us had turned eighteen. My brothers and I knew we would either sign up for the military or attend college. Justin wanted no parts of either, so we tried to get him to prospect for the club once he graduated. He told us he would think about it, but we knew he wouldn't. Justin had told us many times that he planned to get as far away from here as possible when he aged out. And he did. Hell, the diploma was probably still warm in his hands when he left.

"When I asked you what brought you here from Vegas, you said it was because you visited the area, liked Shades Valley, and decided to move and build a practice here. I never thought to ask what brought you to Washington to begin with. I just assumed... Hell, I don't even know what I assumed. I know it's a small fucking world." I picked my beer back up, guzzled the room temperature liquid while I processed the new information. My woman was a vault when it came to sharing anything personal. When she did share, it seemed to be the bare minimum.

I watched Gabriella swipe at the tears on her cheeks, then she sighed and said, "I did not know. It really is a small world. Justin told me about growing up in the foster care system and his parents' death, but he never talked much about the other families he lived with. I came to Washington and visited where he was born, which was Gransville. The only other place he mentioned was Shades Valley. I probably remember it because when he mentioned it, he said his time living here had been the best. I assumed he had finally been placed in a home where the people actually cared for him. He mentioned no one or the family he lived with or why it was the best for him. Just that it had been."

"Damn, I really owe the man. Because of him, I have you and Sawyer. You wouldn't have come here if he hadn't moved to Vegas," I said and shook my head at how life worked sometimes.

"Max, the bike—"

"Yeah, he left on it. I don't figure he still had it when he met you. We might have rebuilt and replaced parts, which was enough for him to ride around here. But with the trip to Vegas, surely the bike hadn't lasted much longer after he had gotten there. We're better now at building and rebuilding them than we were at seventeen." I chuckled, then asked, "Did he buy a new one?"

"No, he loved that bike. I never understood why until now. I stored the bike in my dad's garage. After he died, I couldn't bring myself to get rid of it."

"Wait until I tell the others all this. They'll be surprised, but what will really shock them is that you have the first bike we ever rebuilt together. That bike was where we got the idea of opening a shop one day. Just damn," I said and pull Gabriella closer. "We really need to work on your sharing information about yourself. It isn't like you would be giving up information detrimental to the nation's security." I laughed, and she elbowed me.

"Well, it isn't as if I intentionally withheld the information about Justin. In my defense, though, growing up, my dad would tell us that there was no reason for everyone around us to know every detail about us. My dad stressed it constantly to me and my brother and sister to watch what was said to others, even if we considered them close friends. Hell, even other family members if the information didn't involve them directly or wasn't life or death."

I gave her a brief squeeze. "Hell, your dad sounds so much like mine and the brothers' dads that if I didn't know better, I would think you grew up around an MC… or maybe the mob," I said the last and laughed. When I noticed Gabriella just stared at me instead of laughing along, my laughter died as quickly as it had started.

"Angel, seriously," I said, then let my head fall back against the couch. I raised my free hand up and pinched the bridge of my nose with my finger and thumb. After a few seconds, I dropped my hand and raised my head to look down at her. "You said your dad managed a casino."

She started picking at my shirt as if she were removing lint. "He does for my uncle... Marco Tanucci."

I placed a finger under her chin and lifted her face until she looked at me. "Marco Tanucci, *the* Boss of the Tanucci family in Las Vegas, is your uncle?" I asked.

"Yes," she answered, and I dropped my hand away from her face and laughed. I laughed so hard my eye watered. "Shush, or you're going to wake Sawyer."

I rubbed my hand down my face and worked on getting myself under control. When I sobered up, I shifted both of us until we faced each other on the couch. I placed a hand on each of her cheeks, then leaned forward and gave her a soft kiss.

"Oh, Angel, we are *definitely* going to work on your communication skills," I stated and smiled.

"It's not like I wouldn't have told you before you met my family," she groused. "And I don't know why you were laughing."

"Because the first thing that ran through my mind was that our wedding would be anything but boring," I told her and watched the expression change on her face. "Don't look so worried. I'm sure everyone will behave during the ceremony. Now the reception, well, what could happen between a bunch of bikers and mobsters in the same room with an endless supply of booze?" Gabriella planted her face on my shoulder, and I wrapped my arms around her as my body shook from laughing.

Chapter Twenty-Three

Flirt

Gabriella brushed her teeth and glared at me in the mirror as I leaned against the wall behind her and tapped the box I held in one hand into the palm of my other hand.

She rinsed her mouth out, ran her toothbrush under the water, then placed it in the holder with enough force I was surprised it didn't crack the ceramic. She turned and snatched the box out of my hand.

"No need to be testy."

"Oh, shut up and get out. No way I'm going to pee with you standing over me."

I pushed away from the wall and turned toward the door, mainly so she wouldn't see my lips twitching. I figured it was in my best interest not to mention she had no problem peeing in front of me any other time we'd been in the bathroom together.

"You might as well get it over with and verified with a plus sign so you can set your appointment up with Mac. You've thrown up nine days out of the last fourteen, and you haven't had a period since you moved in here almost two months ago."

"Once it's verified, I won't be able to deny it. I don't even want to know—how you know—I haven't had a period," she said, her voice a tad higher.

Probably would have been a good idea not to have spoken at all.

When I was out of the bathroom, I turned and grabbed the door handle, intending to pull the door shut. Gabriella sat on the toilet, her pajama bottoms around her ankles with the toes of her fuzzy slippers sticking out. She ripped the packaging to get to the stick inside.

I grinned at the sight. "Would you rather wait around seven more months until she or he walks out on their own to make it real?" I grinned when she tried to throw the empty, weightless box at me. It fluttered to the floor less than a foot away from her. "Were you this crazy with Sawyer?"

Yes, it seemed as if I wasn't going to be able to keep my mouth shut.

Dark brown eyes snapped in my direction, and I actually ran my hands over the hairs on my arms to see if they were singed.

"Don't ever… ever… bring up being crazy to a pregnant woman," she said, then used her teeth to tear the flimsy plastic wrap from around the stick. At least that's what I thought she was doing as I pulled the door shut on her mumbled, "Idiot men. The female praying mantis has the right idea—sex—then bite the male's head off and consume him. No body, no jail time."

Christ, I hadn't remembered Sami, Luna, Bailey, or River acting as if they were possessed in the early stage of their pregnancies. Okay, maybe Luna. But the thought of sleeping the next few months with one eye open crossed my mind as I looked down at my watch, then back at the closed door and wondered how long the test would take to show the results.

If my brothers and I had been told when we began returning to the MC from the military that we would take ol' ladies and start having kids before we hit the two-year mark of taking over the club, they would have had to bury us because we would have died from laughing so hard.

I stopped pacing when the bathroom door opened. Gabriella stood in the doorway, and I wondered if it was safe to speak.

"How long until we know for sure?" I asked, since I enjoyed living dangerously, and tried to read the expression on Gabriella's face.

"The package said between two to ten minutes for the results to show up." She leaned her shoulder against the bathroom doorframe, looked at me, and shook her head. "I bet a million dollars your sperm count is well above average. I'm surprised I hadn't felt the little guys swimming and pushing each other out of the way to get to my egg. I set the test on the edge of the counter while I pulled my sleep pants up and washed my hands. Then I glanced over and the plus sign was already forming."

I calculated the chance of her strangling me and started toward her when a smile spread across her face.

"By my calculations, I either became pregnant in the shower when we didn't use a condom or two seconds after I stopped taking my birth control pills, which was only a few days later. So, either way, you, Max Browning, are one potent man and soon-to-be dad."

"You mean, again," I said as I reached Gabriella, wrapped my arms around her, and hugged her as I lifted her off her feet. "I told you before that I may not have been there when Sawyer was born, but it doesn't make her any less mine. She will always be first. I have the documents to prove it. Are you really okay with this, Angel?" I questioned as I set her back on her feet.

"I'm more than okay with it, Max. I'm sorry I acted that way before and placed any doubt in your mind that I wasn't happy about carrying your child. I wish I could promise you there won't be any more crazy episodes, but it would be a lie." Gabriella grinned, and I kissed her forehead.

"Mom? Are you and Dad up?" Sawyer asked from the other side of our bedroom door.

"Yes. Come on in, sweetie," Gabriella answered, and we both turned as the door opened.

"Can I have eggs for breakfast? The soft ones so I can dip my toast in the middle and the yolk runs out?" Sawyer asked as she walked into the bedroom.

Gabriella opened her mouth as if to answer, but instead slapped a hand over her mouth and ran into the bathroom.

Sawyer frowned and asked, "What's wrong with Mom?"

I held up a finger to Sawyer, then entered the bathroom. I grabbed a washcloth and wet it with cold water, and after I set it down on the edge of the counter, I moved behind Gabriella. She was kneeling and bent over the toilet as I reached for her hair with one hand and pulled it back from her face. With my other hand, I rubbed up and down her back as I cringed at the retching sounds.

When it sounded like she was done, at least I hoped, I snagged the cloth and held it down to her. "Here, Angel," I said, and once she had taken the cloth from my hand, I backed up enough to allow her room to sit back on her heels.

After she used the cloth to wipe her face, I helped her stand, and she immediately went to the sink to repeat her earlier tooth brushing process. She turned around, and when I opened my arms, she walked into them.

"Lord, no one is to say the word e-g-g in this house again. Or at least until after the baby arrives. We'll play it by ear then."

"Not sure how that is going to go over. Sawyer loves bacon and e..." The rest of my words were cut off by the hand Gabriella covered my mouth with.

"Don't say it," Gabriella scolded, then dropped her hand from my mouth and stepped out of my arms. "You and Sawyer are just going to have to deal with something else for breakfast until it passes in a couple of months. Hopefully."

"What do you mean, hopefully?" I asked on our way out of the bathroom.

"Morning sickness usually only lasts the first trimester, but there is always a chance it could last the entire pregnancy," Gabriella said as we stepped into the bedroom.

"I'm getting a sister and brother!" Sawyer yelled, practically vibrating where she stood. Gabriella and I both had forgotten she was in the room.

"It looks that way, but you are going to have to settle for one. Twins don't run in our family, sweetie," Gabriella answered, and I smiled when Sawyer walked over and hugged her mother's waist. After she let go of Gabriella, she did the same with me.

"Are you happy, baby girl?" I asked as I hugged her back.

"I am now," she said and smiled before she turned toward the door that led out of the room.

I glanced at Gabriella, who was frowning, and she shrugged. "Why weren't you happy before?" I asked and tried to think of anything that would have Sawyer unhappy because I would fix it.

"I just really wanted a baby brother or sister because Ally is going to get another one," she said on her way out the door.

"Sawyer, you mean because she already has one," Gabriella corrected.

Sawyer stopped and turned around. "I know, and she's getting another one and a cousin, too. I heard Sami and Carly talking about it," Sawyer said, and the look she gave Gabriella and I could only be construed as 'what do you not understand?' then walked out of the room.

I looked at Gabriella and grinned. "Well, it seems you aren't going to be pregnant alone. Though we might want to check if the hospital will assign a delivery room just for Black Hawk births. Round three should start in, I would say... seven months give or take."

"I am thrilled for Carly and Crusher; I know they have been trying for a while. And you know I'm happy for us and Speed and Sami, too. But Max... I am not drinking another thing at Sami and Speed's house," she said and giggled.

I snorted. "I don't think Sami being knocked up again has anything to do with the water at their house. More as if Sami is with Speed like you are with me—can't go without our dic—"

"If you finish that, I will show you how long I can go without it," she said and walked out of the bedroom.

I caught up to her in the hallway and threw my arm over her shoulders. I leaned my head closer to hers, so my lips were at her ear. "Later at Whispering Nights, I think I'll test how long you can go before you're begging for my dick," I whispered, dropped my arm from her shoulder, and started down the stairs.

"Sometimes you are a pain in my ass," she said so low I almost hadn't heard her.

"Want me to show you later how true I can make that?" I answered as I reached the bottom of the stairs, then burst out laughing when a fuzzy slipper flew past my head.

Epilogue One

Flirt

Seven months later…

Christ, I had witnessed and done things in the military that left marks on my soul, but watching my woman in pain as she struggled to bring our son into the world had stripped every nerve and kicked all rationality to the curb.

"Goddammit, Mac, can't you do something!"

"Am I going to have to call security to drag your ass out of here? Everything is great and going as it should," Mac said, and I saw her roll her eyes at Gabriella.

Gabriella leaned back on the pillow and looked up at me. "Max, it's okay if you need to step out for a minute."

"What the hell, Gabriella? I am not going anywhere. And if anyone even thinks about throwing me out, they better have their life insurance paid up." I looked pointedly at Mac, not caring that she was a brother's ol' lady. Later, when Coast punched me, I would deal.

"Mac, I am so sorry," Gabriella said, which had my head jerking in her direction instead of glaring at Mac.

"Why are you apologizing to her? She's the one sitting calmly on the stool doing nothing to help with your pain."

"Doing good, Brie. Next contraction should do it. I want you to bear down hard. Let's get this little guy out before his daddy has a nervous breakdown."

I watched Gabriella nod, then saw the pain in her eyes as her breathing picked up, then she squeezed my hand. I supported her back when she rose, and then her eyes closed as she did what Mac had asked of her. She went from bearing down to a scream that ripped my heart out. I opened my mouth and was prepared to rip into Mac when the crying penetrated my ears.

I helped as Gabriella relaxed back into the bed, kissed her forehead, and when I turned, Mac was laying Ethan on Gabriella's stomach. I cut the cord and continued to watch in a daze as Mac did her thing, then wrapped a cloth around him.

"Let's get him weighed and measured and cleaned up, and we'll bring him right back," Mac said and handed him off to the waiting nurse beside her.

She went back to taking care of Gabriella, then when she was done, she walked across the room to where the nurse had Ethan.

I ran my hand over Gabriella's head and watched as they dealt with Ethan. His cry was acknowledgement of his unhappy state. Mac turned with Ethan in her arms and walked toward me.

"Here you go, Daddy. Say hi to your son. We'll let you hold him a second, then you can pass him off to Mom and she can see if he is interested in nursing," Mac said and smiled when I reached out and took him into my arms.

"Thank you, Angel," I said vehemently.

"Anytime. Well, after maybe a year or so," Gabriella answered, and both Mac and I chuckled. I kissed Ethan's forehead and passed him off to Gabriella, who already had her gown pushed aside exposing her breast to see if the little guy would nurse.

I watched, amazed as he rutted around her breast. "Going to be a breast man for sure," I said.

Mac snorted. "Is there a man who isn't?"

"Not sure, but his interest verifies he belongs to me." I grinned when Gabriella looked at me and rolled her eyes.

"Ethan's color, lungs, toes, fingers, and his heart all look and sound great. I won't even get upset when you unwrap him and check for yourself. He weighs eight pounds even and measured twenty-two inches long. You did an awesome job, Brie. He is gorgeous," Mac said as she observed Ethan trying his best to find the food source.

Ethan's face reddened, and he let out a cry of frustration. Gabriella helped him and his little mouth finally found her nipple and latched on.

"Excellent. Good to see he isn't going to have to be coaxed. Some newborns fight it and the mothers get frustrated," Mac injected.

"Sawyer was the same. I never had a problem breastfeeding her," Gabriella stated.

"Oh my God, I forgot to tell you that while you were getting prepped for delivery, Carly's water broke in the waiting area. Seems I'm going to have a busy night," Mac said and shook her head.

"How's Crusher hanging in?" I asked, and Gabriella eyed me as if to say 'really.'

"He was doing great, cool and calm. At least when I left him with Carly. Not sure what kind of shape he'll be in when I get back in there. When I was leaving the room, she was already saying that she was going to shoot him. If Crusher doesn't sleep with one eye open, he is as crazy as she is," Mac said and laughed.

I realized both women knew why I asked. I wanted Crusher to be acting semi-nuts like I had. Though, like Mac had pointed out, the man lived with Carly.

"Thanks, Mac, for everything. You know I didn't mean all the stuff I said before," I apologized.

"Please, I'm getting kind of used to it with you guys. Besides, if you are yelling and complaining, it means you are still standing and breathing. It would surprise you at the number of dads who spend the delivery of their child on the floor." At Mac's words, the nurse across the room snorted.

"When can Sawyer come in?" Gabriella asked.

"We're going to give you a few minutes together, then you'll be taken to a room. If you need anything before a nurse checks back in or I do, buzz for help. I'm going to go check on Carly really quick, then I'll swing by the waiting area and let everyone know Ethan has arrived. I'll bring Sawyer with me when I head back in this direction. Let you guys spend some time as a family before the others converge," Mac said and turned toward the door.

"Hey, Mac, any chance Carly and Gabriella can share a room like Sami and Luna did? It sure would save everyone from going back and forth between two rooms," I mentioned.

Mac looked over her shoulder and grinned. "Please, that was done before they finished mopping Carly's water off the floor," Mac said and laughed as she pulled the door open and walked out with the nurse.

I rested a hip on the side of the bed and leaned my upper body on the mattress next to Gabriella, facing her with my one arm curved over her head. "I love you, Angel," I said as I let a strand of her hair fall through my fingers and listened to her talk softly to our son.

"Love you more, Max."

"Angel, I don't think that's possible." I laid my head beside hers on the pillow. "Turning around and following you back into Whispering Nights was the best decision I ever made."

Gabriella adjusted and cradled Ethan with one arm, then turned her head so we were face to face. She raised the freed hand and placed it on the side of my face. Then she used her thumb and caressed my cheek.

"Yes, it was," she said and smiled. "I'll be thankful for the rest of my life."

I smiled and kissed her on her nose. When she turned her head back to our son, I closed my eyes and sighed.

Before long, a nurse came in and they moved Gabriella to a semi-private room. No sooner than she and Ethan were settled, the door opened and Sawyer walked in, holding Mac's hand.

"Delivering a little girl eager to meet her brother," Mac said as they entered, and she let go of Sawyer's hand.

"Whoa," I said just in time to stop Sawyer from diving on the bed.

"Is he sleeping? Can I hold him? How come he isn't crying? The other babies do," she asked with her litany of questions. I grinned and lifted her so she could get a good look at her brother.

"Here, sweetie, you can sit beside me and I'll let you hold him," Gabriella said and scooted over, making room for Sawyer to sit beside her on the bed.

I sat her down on the bed, then Gabriella placed Ethan in Sawyer's arms with her own arms helping to support him. They had their dark-haired heads together, looking down at Ethan.

It was at that moment I really understood the meaning behind Coast's words when we were standing in Sami and Luna's hospital room.

"When it's right you don't feel as if you've given up anything. But you are aware of everything you've gained." I had gained a lot. So much, I imagined life couldn't get much better.

Of course, life proved me wrong two years later with Liam's birth.

Epilogue Two

Tracker

Several years later…

It was still dark as I took in my surroundings and walked my bike toward the front of the house. The house I had lived in when my brother, Paxton, and I had left the reservation with the couple who took us on and gave us a place to live. I had been twelve and Paxton seven when we came to the Black Hawk MC compound.

What we'd found with the couple was a home, love, and a family. They had even added a brother when they adopted Eli from the reservation, the same as they had done for us.

I turned the corner of the house and stopped. I pushed the kickstand down and stared at the five men who stood side-by-side, blocking my way.

"What are you doing out here so early?" I asked, then turned my head at the sound of the front door opening. My dad walked out and down the few stairs and joined the others.

"You didn't think we would let you pull out of here without saying goodbye, did you, kid?" Speed said.

"Hell, he looks better leaving than he did when he first showed up," Crusher said.

"He sure was scrawny. A strong wind would have blown him and Paxton away that day," Devil added.

"Only difference now is he has more height, but no meat," Jag said.

"Give the Army time. They'll beef him up," Flirt answered.

"He's working on that himself if my grocery bill while he's been here is any sign," my dad, Coast, spoke, and I noticed he held a box in his hands.

"Really, you guys didn't have to get up. I didn't expect you to," I said and looked at each man. Then I looked at my dad and added. "And I just told you and Mom goodbye in the house."

"Be glad you had your leather jacket on. At least this time you don't have to wear a wet shirt for a couple hours like you did when you left for BT (Basic Training)," my dad said.

I chuckled. "It took three hours for my shirt to dry when I left. I didn't know a woman could cry that many tears. She bawled at my graduation from BT. Then bawled even more when you and she came to my graduation from AIT (Advanced Individual Training). I think she has cried every day since I have been home on leave."

"Cut your mom a break. She's having a rough time accepting that you're not only an adult, but you've chosen to go into the military. I think she was hoping you would stay and work with us at the bike shop." My dad tried to explain.

"I get it. Maybe she'll be better the next time I come home on leave," I said and shifted on my seat. "Well, I probably should get going. I've got a lot of riding from here to Texas."

"Don't push it. You have plenty of time before you need to report. When you stop for the night, call me," my dad said, then he glanced at the others.

"Before you leave, though, we have something for you. Should've done it yesterday when the entire club was here for your sendoff party, but we decided we wanted it to be a little more private," Crusher said, and then my dad held out the box he had been holding.

"I don't know if I have room in my saddlebags for anything else," I said as I took the box and rested it on my bike in front of me so I could lift the lid.

"I'll keep it at the house for you," my dad answered.

I frowned as I lifted the lid off the box. Then froze with the top in my hands and stared at what was revealed.

"Are you going to stare at it, or are you going to pull it out and look at it?" My dad asked and took the lid to free up my hands.

"I have a vest," I said as I reached for the neatly folded leather cut.

"A plain one with only your name stitched on. Pull it out," Crusher said, and I lifted the vest out and unfolded it. The back held the club patch in the center and a rocker underneath with Shades Valley, Washington, stitched on it. The rocker on top had Prospect. When I turned it around, my name was the only thing on the front left side. I looked up, and my dad and the others smiled.

"There's no time limit on when you wear it. It's more so you know the Black Hawk MC will always be at your back, whether you are in the military and stationed around the world or home on the compound. You need us—we're there," Crusher said.

My dad placed his hand on my shoulder and squeezed as I worked to swallow the lump that had formed in my throat.

I folded the cut and set it back in the box, and after my dad placed the lid back on, he picked it up. I dismounted my bike and moved to stand in front of the men who had accepted me from the moment I stepped foot on the grounds of the compound. Almost in the same spot where we stood.

"I don't know where Paxton and I would have ended up if we hadn't met you that day in the clinic. When we went back with the social worker, I never figured I'd see you again. Even when you showed up with Mom at the social worker's office, I was afraid to hope that you had come for us," I said to my dad, then looked at each of the other men and continued. "Then we got out of the car, and all of you were there to welcome us, and you have never stopped. You proved what loyalty means, and that family isn't defined by the blood running in your veins. I can't imagine meeting any men greater than what I have grown up around."

"Goddamn, kid. Are you trying to make everyone on this compound cry?" my dad asked as he grabbed me and gave me a one-armed hug.

Each man embraced me, and when it was over, I got back on my bike. I didn't crank it until I was on the road in front of the house. Before I pulled away, I looked over my shoulder at my dad and the others one last time, then twisted the throttle putting my bike in motion.

I glanced around as I rolled down the road taking everything in, not wanting to forget anything about the place while I was away. As I reached the front of Speed's house, I caught movement out of the corner of my eye and looked up. In the upstairs window, Ally stood. I gave a chin lift, and received a small smile back, then kicked the bike up a notch and headed for the gate.

I didn't know exactly where life and the military would take me or what would happen along the way. However, I knew that no matter what took place, it would always bring me back to the Black Hawk MC—my home.

Epilogue Three

Stroker
(with the other dads)

More years later...

I watched the Black Hawk MC members and their families eating, laughing, and enjoying themselves, then looked around at my closest friends and brothers.

"When we left the military and started the club, did you ever envision any of this?" I stretched out my arm and waved my hand to encompass everyone at the club's Fourth of July barbecue.

"No. And the only thing that would make this better is if Cutter was here to enjoy it with us," Flyboy said and the other men and I nodded in agreement.

I shook my head, remembering our friend and brother whose life was cut short. "Can you imagine if he was? Christ, the three boys of Speed's would be meaner. And that's saying something compared to how they already are. I will admit, though, the best part would have been watching Ally wrap the tough bastard around her finger."

"Oh yeah. Now that would have been enjoyable to watch," Romeo said.

"Even after all this time I don't think a day passes that I don't think of him," I said, and the others acknowledged the same. "I'll admit the thought of him with Carly and Crusher's boys... what a nightmare. It has nothing to do with how I would have had to share the boys with Cutter. They just don't need any more encouragement than they already get. I love my grandsons, but they are already hoodlums at six and seven. I don't know if any of us will survive their teenage years. The other day Crusher mentioned he and Carly were setting up college funds for the boys, and he got pissed when I mentioned that maybe a bail fund would be a better idea. Those boys will more than likely need that before college money."

"Then it's probably a good thing their mama's the sheriff," Will, River's dad and recently retired county sheriff, said as he walked up and sat down to join us. When Will had announced his retirement, Carly ran for the position. I wasn't sure who was more shocked, her or the club, when she won by a landslide.

"Hell, I'm not sure being their mama will stop her from locking 'em up. The woman has a mean streak a mile long and wide," Roscoe said, and we all turned and looked at him. "What? Every one of ya knows she's mean. You want to talk about if Cutter was still alive and how his influence would have affected his grandkids. For fuck's sake, imagine Cutter with Carly. It is right sad he never got to meet his daughter, but if he had, that father and daughter combo would keep your asses up at night."

Romeo snorted. "You're just mad Carly pulled you over last week and read you the riot act," he said, and earned a glare from Roscoe while the rest of us chuckled.

"Well, there was no reason for it. Damn sure wasn't a reason for her yelling that she should write me up for recklessness. I hit a goddamn oil spot on the road. Not like I didn't get the bike back under control," Roscoe said in a put-out tone.

I stopped grinning, ran my hand across the back of my neck, and took a deep breath. It was the perfect opening for the subject I had been elected to talk to Roscoe about. I felt eyes on me and knew the others were thinking the same thing. Even knowing they would have my back didn't make it any easier for me to broach the subject.

"Yeah, Carly mentioned it took you a bit to straighten out the bike," I started, but didn't get anything else out before Roscoe bristled and cut in.

"For fuck's sake, I got it under control. That's what matters. I've been riding longer than the girl's been alive. She doesn't know what she's talking about, and she should mind her own—"

"Stop it! Your old ass scared the shit out of her, Roscoe," I blurted out, cutting his rant off. No man wanted to admit that age was slowing them down.

"What?" he said with a little less steam than he previously had in his words.

"You scared her, brother," I repeated, then continued. "She watched the bike come loose in the curve and there was nothing she could do about it. She figured she was going to have a front row seat to you crashing. I was at her and Crusher's house when she walked in." I shook my head, remembering. "Crusher asked her what happened, and that was all it took to break her down. I have never seen the girl so torn up. I can count on one hand the times I've witnessed her crying but nothing like that day."

"She didn't act upset when she pulled me over. She acted pissed. She started yelling at me about slowing my

239

fucking ass down because she didn't have time to waste standing around while they scraped me off the road," Roscoe said, then I watched him look down at his hands and flex them.

"Is your arthritis acting up?" Dare asked as he joined us and sat down beside Roscoe.

Roscoe blew out a breath before he answered, "Yeah, the damn stuff is getting worse. Flaring up more every dang day. Already taking the max dosage in medication to ease it. Doc said if it gets worse, he's going to have to change my medication again. Getting old sucks ass, boys. Some days, it takes all I can do to get my hands to cooperate enough so I can squeeze Sue's ass."

Several of us chuckled, and a few groaned. There wasn't one of us at the table who couldn't relate to how Roscoe felt. No biker wanted to acknowledge his riding days were limited. I already knew I would prolong it if I possibly could.

Hell, there were already more days than not when I got off my bike after a ride and my legs hurt, my hands ached, and my ass was numb. I even wondered if I was going to walk the next day. Yet it never stopped me from getting back on my bike. Nothing came close to the feeling of riding the open road with the wind hitting me. I would do whatever it took to keep experiencing it.

"I'm sure the boys could modify your roadster into a trike," Preacher suggested. The look Roscoe gave him had my lips twitching, and when I looked at the others, they were in the same shape. Every one of us was fighting to contain our laughter.

"Fuck every one of you bastards. You bunch of assholes," was out of Roscoe's mouth no sooner than Preacher had finished speaking, and the control we were desperately holding onto collapsed, and laughter filled the air.

"Laugh now, but it will happen to all your asses sooner rather than later." That added statement from Roscoe sobered everyone.

Roscoe didn't have that many years on me and the others who were sitting around him.

None of us said anything for a few minutes. I imagined the others were like me and prayed for many more years to pass before any of us had to face the same decision as Roscoe.

"Ya know, I'm not ashamed to admit there are days I wish we were still the small club from the beginning," Romeo said, bringing us back to the initial conversation about the club and off the depressing crap of aging.

"Well, it sure was a lot quieter back then," Preacher added and grinned.

"Hell, I can't remember what quiet is," Flyboy replied as laughter and yelling filled the air around us. Each of us turned toward the noise in time to watch a water balloon hit Luna's shoulder and explode.

"For fuck's sake, do those kids have death wishes?" I asked, not expecting an answer as we watched the start of a water war between the women and their sons.

"Never thought back in the day when the condoms had been tampered with that the result would look like that," Cruz said, lifted his chin to point toward the large group scattered in front of us, then he slid over to make room for Thelma when she approached with Willa, Sue, Shakes, and Claire. The five women had been in the clubhouse's kitchen dealing with the food for the barbeque.

Thelma snorted as she and the other four women sat. "What makes you think it's the end? They might not add to their families. Maybe they are just taking a break."

"Jesus, woman, bite your tongue. They need to be finished. As it stands now, the club doesn't have to worry

241

about recruiting new prospects anytime soon. It's as if our boys are running their own MC farming program," Cruz said.

I chuckled because Cruz really wasn't far off with all the boys added to the families over the years. Crusher and Carly, along with Flirt and Brie, and Jag and River, had two boys each. Speed and Sami, Devil and Bailey, Ghost and Luna, and Coast and Mac added three sons a piece to the mix. Eighteen boys between the seven couples. It guaranteed Black Hawk MC's survival for years to come. The only boy absent at the cookout was Tracker, who was currently entering phase four of the SFQC (Special Forces Qualification Course). He had joined the military right after he graduated high school. He was the oldest of the grandchildren at twenty-two.

Flyboy, Romeo, Preacher, Cruz, Cutter, and I had come to Shades Valley after leaving the military intending to start an MC. What it had grown into, though, exceeded our expectations in a big way. But our choice to step down out of the leadership roles when our boys found their way home after their own military stints had been the best decision for the club and them.

"I think you are forgetting about a few other children," Willa said and touched my arm, bringing me out of my thoughts.

"What, sweetheart?" I asked, then leaned closer and kissed her cheek. The pinkish blush that appeared on her cheeks made me smile. Even after several years together, she was still easily embarrassed at any level of affection displayed publicly.

"I think Willa's referring to those four. When you men count, you always leave out the girls," Sue said and drew everyone's attention.

I looked to where she was pointing to see sixteen-year-olds Ally and Sawyer, stepping around the corner of the clubhouse with fourteen-year-old Neely and eleven-year-old Poppy bringing up the rear. Ally had the nozzle of a hose in her hand as Neely was unraveling it as they moved around the clubhouse. Once they reached the backdoor, Sawyer grabbed the nozzle to the water hose connected to the back wall while Poppy started uncurling it.

"Oh hell, I'll tell ya right now nothing good is coming from that shit," Roscoe said, and I had to agree as we watched Ally lean over and turn the knob that opened the flow of water. All four girls focused on the group still running around screaming and laughing as water balloons were launched.

The water fight was raging with the boys ganging up on their mothers, soaking them while Crusher, Ghost, Devil, Speed, Jag, Flirt, and Coast cheered the boys on from the picnic table they sat around. Somehow, the men seemed to have stayed dry through it all. Not one of them had a wet spot showing on any area of their clothing.

At least in that round.

"Think we outta give the boys a heads up?" Cruz asked and chuckled. "It would be the fatherly thing to do."

"Probably would be the adult thing to do, too. But do you think they'd give us a warning if we were the ones who were going to be ambushed?" Flyboy asked.

Everyone was quiet as we watched the four girls move undetected toward their unsuspecting targets. By the time the men received any notice as they dragged the hoses across the yard, the girls were almost within reach of their prey. With a few more steps, twin sprays of water were cut loose, and the yelling of curse words had everyone in the surrounding area turning in the table's direction.

I shook my head and laughed with the others at the men who sat there with water dripping off them from the attack.

Ally and the other three girls dropped the hoses and doubled over laughing. When the men stood and moved, the girls screamed and took off running.

"I swear, the four of them cause more trouble than the boys combined," Claire spoke for the first time.

Shakes snickered, "That's a fact. Just imagine them as grown women. The world better get prepared for the four of them to be cut loose in it."

"World? We should be scared for the poor men who cross their paths," Thelma said and laughed with the other women.

I looked at the women and men around me. "The thought of how much trouble those girls are going to stir up as adults is incomprehensible, but it sure as shit will be fun as hell watching it play out."

"While we are waiting for that to happen, anyone up for a little bet?" Dare asked.

"A bet on what?" I questioned.

"Even though Ally caused the cussing by hosing them. Anyone want to bet she'll make them pay for all the bad words they spouted?" Dare concluded, and the entire group howled until we were wiping tears from our eyes. I doubt anyone knew how much money the girl had stashed.

Yes indeed, watching the next generation of the Black Hawk MC would be interesting.

A Note from Carson

I want to thank everyone for their interest in my guys. It was hard writing Flirt's story, knowing he was the last of the Black Hawk MC's sons to find his ol' lady. I have loved the writing journey each of them has taken me on, even though, along the way, they sometimes fought and argued with me.

Flirt was a struggle, resulting in delays. I know everyone wanted his story and wondered if it was ever going to be released. Normally, I would apologize for the delays, not this time. Flirt's story needed to be the best I could give not only to him, but to myself.

As authors, our characters are family, and we want what is best for them. We go into stories, understanding that some readers will enjoy it while others will not. However, we need to be satisfied with the end result of a book. I feel I have given my best to Flirt and can move on with satisfaction.

What I can't do—is leave two of the dads alone. So… there will be a novella—keep an eye out for Flyboy & Preacher—a sort of catchup book for the group while the dads take a little of the spotlight.

As far as the Black Hawk MC is concerned, I refuse to

say goodbye to them. I have a feeling they will pop up in the future—a few ideas are brewing. 😊

Carson

Acknowledgments

Thank you to everyone who invested their time reading the Black Hawk MC.

Carson

About the Author

Carson lives in the South with a Great Dane and two adopted shelter dogs that keep the household in line. Books have always been a part of her life. There is nothing better to her than curling up and relaxing with a good story and losing herself in someone else's world for a few hours.

She enjoys writing romance with a real feel to the stories. Writing with the belief not every man is a jerk and not every woman needs saving.

Writing and growing as an author with each book is her goal. She wants to reach the level where a reader knows when they see her name, they can trust there will be a good story as they flip through the pages.

Carson's been on her writing journey for a few years. As she's finally settling in, her only regret is she hadn't started sooner.

Books by Carson Mackenzie

Black Hawk MC

Speed
Crusher
Devil
Ghost
Jag
Coast
Flirt

Haven MC

Moose's Regret
Hawk's Bounty
Keg's Revelation

Desert Phoenix MC

Desert Phoenix Rising

Standalones

Her Way or No Way
two paths One destiny

Boxed Sets

Black Hawk MC Books 1-3
Black Hawk MC Books 4-7
Haven MC Books 1-3

www.ingramcontent.com/pod-product-compliance
Lightning Source LLC
Chambersburg PA
CBHW022107240626
47153CB00007B/2268